I0817830

ELEPHANT AND RABBIT

AS TOLD BY SKIB BRICLUSTER

Also by T. A. Young

The Fairy Tale Book
of Bifford C. Wellington

ELEPHANT AND RABBIT

AS TOLD BY SKIB BRICLUSTER

T. A. Young

138 In Progress Publishing
New York

138 In Progress Publishing
Dover Plains, New York
www.138inprogresspublishing.com

Elephant And Rabbit As Told By Skib Bricluster

Art production provided by theodore gallmeyer.
www.verticalpen.com

Edited by Marian Grudko

Library of Congress Control Number: 2016917709
ISBN: 978-0-9982768-0-9

Printed in the United States of America
Second Edition: June 2017

This book is dedicated to

Mrs. Malubier
Victrola Anne
Taylor Maximus

CONTENTS

ILLUSTRATIONS

We'll always find something, eh Didi,
to give us the impression we exist?

— Samuel Beckett,
Waiting for Godot

"No, no! The adventures first,"
said the Gryphon in an impatient tone,
"explanations take such a dreadful time."

— Lewis Carroll

Elephant and Rabbit
As Told By Skib Bricluster

When creatures of the magic forest spoke of The Rabbit, they knew exactly which one they were talking about. He was the one who had defeated the crafty old Witch of the Red Woods; who had outrun Rupert Panther for the Golden Twig; who had sung the Orange Prippit to sleep and returned the Cape of Wonder that had been stolen from Little Hannah Bat; and who had most recently wrestled Morgan Weasel into early retirement. This was some rabbit.

One morning Rabbit – and from here on, when we say "Rabbit" we mean "The Rabbit" – stepped out of his warren, took a deep breath, and saw the sky move, not in the usual graceful way, but lumbering, almost awkward. He thought he must have eaten a bad carrot: how else to explain this strange vision?

The wall of grey swung towards Rabbit and he saw the head of the creature that was a mountain. The tusks, ears, and trunk were too much to take in. Rabbit was used to seeing the usual magical forest fare; and, really, until the magic gets involved, it's all pretty run-of-the-mill stuff. Sure, the odd giant, but giants were merely enormous people. The occasional troll, but trolls were merely small, squishy, grotesque, foul smelling people. And witches, who really were people. Then it was all rabbits and frogs and robins and crows and bats and squirrels and fish and goblins and such. Never, ever had there been an elephant in the forest.

"How did you get here?" asked Rabbit.

"I took a quick left at the Mailbox of Foreboding."

"Ah, the short cut. What are you?"

"We call ourselves Whooshponders."

"Whooshponders? Listen, I know we just met and you have a couple of kilos on me, but that name is all wrong. All wrong. First of all, one look at you and I can see you do not whoosh. Lumber, yes. Whoosh, no. And "Ponder" should be "Pounder," *n'est-ce pas*? I can see you pounding, but pondering? Okay, what do you characters do?"

If an elephant could shrug with gravity he would have. What he did do was raise his right leg and slam it down. Th earth shook and a nearby tree fell, home of Lanford Robin and family. (The ensuing litigation was an ugly affair.)

"Exactly my point," said Rabbit as his comportment slowly returned to him.

The elephant asked what Rabbit could do.

"I can give you the value of pi to the fourth place."

" I like my trick better."

'So do I."

The next day, over a breakfast of eggs and toast, Rabbit suggested he give the elephant a tour of the forest. And so out they went.

They were having a smacking good time, meeting the flora and fauna of the woods – talking flowers, dancing rocks, singing turtles, cursing trolls, gambling butterflies, drunken badgers, hysterical whooping cranes, belligerent owls, clumsy elves, lying dwarves, bitter fairies, ambivalent gnomes, useless witches, melancholy goblins, disillusioned snails, unemployed pixies, brilliant bats – when they reached the River of Sunlight and Moonbeams. Or Sunbeams and Moonlight. One of those kinds of names.

"What is this?" asked the elephant.

"This is the River of…the River of Somelight!" said Rabbit triumphantly.

"I've never seen such a thing. What does it do?"

"Why, it….it moves along these banks here in that direction" (he pointed in that direction) "and if you go into it, it makes you wet."

"Like rain."

"Like rain, but a lot faster."

The elephant jumped in.

Rabbit went into his hero mode: he would jump into the river, grab the elephant by his tail and drag him out. As he pulled off his shoes he watched the pachyderm float down the river. Float! Rabbit marveled, wondering how such a big thing didn't just sink to the bottom. In fact, the elephant was swimming smoothly and calmly with the current. Rabbit ran along the bank, calling out to him to slow down or turn around or something. The elephant said he was fine and asked where the river led.

"It leads to that direction, for crying out loud." And he pointed more emphatically than before in that direction.

"Well, I think that's where I'll be going, too."

"But..." Rabbit didn't know what to say. He had already grown to like the big galoot and he was sorry to lose him so quickly.

"Will you be back?"

"I don't know. I'm not a real forward thinker." Rabbit was finding it hard to keep up; he ran, stumbling over roots and brush and rocks and naiads doing their laundry.

"I have to tell you, I'm not really comfortable with this. I'm inclined to jump in and save you."

"No need, no need. We float like leaves. We're wonderfully buoyant. Thank you, though."

Still, Rabbit ran and ran, following the elephant until he was completely out of breath. He stopped and watched him drift away, growing smaller and smaller, until he was just another ripple in the river.

Nothing makes a rabbit more philosophical than watching an elephant he has recently befriended float away down a river. A feeling of emptiness struck him.

One day while lolling on a cushiony patch of grass, the soft October sun suddenly disappeared behind an enormous grey cloud. A floppy, leathery grey cloud. And it began to rain…but a lot faster. Rabbit shielded his eyes from this sudden squall, sat up, and found that the elephant had returned, apparently by river. That's called Impressive Navigation.

Their simultaneous smiles were like – Oh, let's just say it! – a rainbow.

*. . . (for on this point the authors
who have written on this subject differ.)*

— Cervantes, *Don Quixote*

Elephant and Rabbit II

One day Rabbit and Elephant were playing around, taking turns giving piggyback rides, when...

Whoa! Whoa! Whoa! Are you telling me that at some time during this playing around, Rabbit was giving Elephant a piggyback ride? Isn't that just a bit incredible? I mean, assuming Rabbit is rabbit-sized and Elephant is pachyderm-sized, and that Rabbit isn't Super Rabbit (that would be his second cousin on his father's side), how is that possible?

Are you finished? What I meant to say is that they were taking turns giving piggyback rides to - See? You should have let me finish - to their friends, Squirrel, Gopher, and Mole. Frankly, it would have been easier for Rabbit to carry Elephant than to carry these guys. Squirrel was all jittery, so he kept hopping on and off of Rabbit's back; Gopher kept getting dizzy and throwing up; and Mole had no idea what was going on: on a back, off a back, it was all the same. In a word: Whatever. But throw a grub his way and watch him very quickly find meaning in life.

Ah, the story.

At one point during these shenanigans, Squirrel took a spill, bouncing a bit before he landed in a bramble bush, which is bad if you're furry, and bad if you're not furry. As he helped himself up, his left foreleg stepped into a pail painted light blue. A rare find in these parts, especially in this condition: very slight rusting, minor paint loss, a couple of small dings, otherwise perfect. What made it especially desirable was the image of the white sailboat stenciled on it.

Need we say that the others were thunder-struck. When they found their voices, Rabbit was the first to speak: "What the heck....Is it a magical thing?...How does it work?" Practical Rabbit.

Squirrel was pretty practical, too, so he placed the pail over his head and waited for something to happen. Then he put the pail on the ground and put his head back in. Then he stood in it with both feet. The others watched with interest and approval; they knew Science when they saw it.

Then Gopher gave it a shot: he smelled it and licked it and bit it and slapped his tail against it inside and out.

Elephant tried to stir the magic using trunk and tail.

Mole climbed into it. Knowing futility when they saw it, they patiently waited for his head to pop up. You know that feeling you get? Well, that was when they peered into the pail and saw nothing. The pail was empty!

"It works!" said Elephant.

"Yep." That was Rabbit. The others – the remaining others – nodded.

"How does he get back?" asked Gopher.

"What if we need another pail?" Elephant asked.

"Yep." Rabbit again.

Time crawled.

"Feels like rain," Gopher said.

They kept looking into the pail.

The sky grew dark: the onset of evening or of rain. Your call.

"Yep." (You know who.)

Suddenly there was a clap of thunder so loud that it shook the forest. The pail fell over and out toppled Mole. The others looked at Mole with relief; he looked remarkably well, thank goodness.

"Why are you looking at me like that?"

"What happened?" asked Elephant.

"What do you mean?"

"Where did you go?"

"What do you mean?"

Luckily, it began to rain. Rabbit grabbed the pail and told the others not to follow him. He headed to Lake Yuck about a half a mile down. When he arrived there, he walked as close to the edge of the lake as he dared, then flung the pail as high and as far as he could. The pail was airborne for about two seconds before it landed three feet from Rabbit. But that was far enough, for the pail did what Rabbit wanted it to do, which was to sink out of sight.

"Magic," he said half aloud.
And he shuddered at the thought.

Here, at the very beginning,
I have to interrupt the thread of my narration
to introduce the reader to the location
of a certain drama.

ANDREI BELY, *PETERSBURG*

Elephant and Rabbit III

We can postulate reasons for Elephant's fondness for the river ; certainly they had had time to get to know each other; each had made a wonderful impression on the other; each had learned the other's language. Talk about immersion.

So Rabbit and Elephant would often lounge by the bank of the river; Rabbit would watch Elephant walk back and forth, raising and lowering his trunk, as he and the river conversed about who-knows-what. As curious as he was, Rabbit was comfortable not sticking his nose in others' business; besides, he could tell it was probably some Zen thing, the universe is one, the voice of silence, being, potential, the now…all good stuff, but Rabbit was – if this makes any sense at all – too laid-back to be Zen: he was a carrots and naps kind of Rabbit. Tough to argue, but why would you?

Then Elephant jumped into the river. Again. Rabbit leaped up, ran to the river, and this time, jumped in, too. The magnitude of this act cannot be overstated: rabbits detest the insides of rivers; as far as rabbits go, all wetness to the fur is to be avoided. But they can swim well and require no training whatsoever to do so. Elephant didn't know this, so he trumpeted in alarm, scooped his friend up, sat him on his back and held him there with his trunk, perhaps a bit too tightly, but he was scared for him.

"Elephant, you can loosen up a bit," said Rabbit.

"Not a chance. You're no Whooshponder."

"I didn't know Whooshponders could swim, you didn't know Rabbits could swim."

"What's your point?"

"No idea. But I am beginning to lose consciousness. A little oxygen would be nice."

Elephant relaxed his grip and they floated along just fine. Rabbit took it all in as they passed the familiar landmarks of the magic forest.

Then things got weird: when all the familiar landmarks were exhausted, they were replaced by unfamiliar stuff that made Rabbit uneasy, maybe simply because it was unfamiliar. Coming from the magic forest, one is not usually rattled by the weird stuff because that's the normal stuff. The problem was the rocks.

These were the rocks that broke the fall of Hephaestus. These were the rocks that held Prometheus to that frozen promontory, before he was released and the rocks fell and fell and fell. These were the rocks that were left over from the formation of the boulder of Sisyphus. These were the remains of the rock that Magor hurled at the Clasttian hordes, decimating their ranks and forcing their retreat. These were the shards of the splintered mountain that held Tratus until his tectonic-plate-cracking escape. These were the residue of the Gorgons' work; bits of Niobe's misery. Some had markings like runes. One had a deep cavity, rectangular and very narrow, as if it held some ancient king's sword. We're talking the time of giants, recall.

They were sharp and dark and their gravity was awesome: these were serious rocks, not playful, cuddly, cutesy little rocks that you see sometimes playing with doilies and parasols and drinking tea out of china cups with their pinky fingers extended. These rocks growled their ferocity; the waters that dared to approach them could muster barely a gurgle.

Rabbit shuddered.

Elephant said, "They're the same color as me."

Rabbit said, "Aye." Or maybe it was "I."

Then of course, as if in collusion, the sky, too, became the color of the rocks. Rabbit suggested they turn back, so Elephant obliged by turning himself around, resulting in a floating-backwards elephant with a backwards facing rabbit on his back, yielding nothing by way of comfort to the rabbit.

Emboldened by his own cowardice – this is called Jungian Enantiodromia – Rabbit announced that he was getting off this ride, insisting that Elephant remove his trunk from his torso. He did, so he did.

Rabbit really showed his grit: it seemed that no matter which direction he took, he was swimming against the current, but he found himself out of the river and again looking at his friend who seemed more in his element now than when he was on land.

But elephant had been down this road before and chose to be with his pal on the bank of the river, and so they found themselves marching back to the magic forest, leaving all that grey stuff....well, most of that grey stuff...behind. Obviously, some of that grey behind went with them.

But all that stuff is what happens before the story, which begins precisely where and when the two come face to face with Rupert Panther, who was still cheesed off about the famous Golden Twig imbroglio that had added to the legend that is Rabbit, and seriously sullied the stature of Rupert, who was simply not a good sport. But that's a Panther thing. When the two came upon him, he was just finishing off a little meal that consisted of another critter that tried to test Rupert's nature.

"Gee, Rupert, you look like you're wearing lipstick," noted Rabbit.

"It's blood, Rabbit."

"It really looks like lipstick. Doesn't it look like he's wearing lipstick, Elephant?"

As comfortable as Elephant was in the river is exactly the opposite of how he was feeling now; he wanted no part of Rupert Panther. Rather, he wanted Rupert Panther to have no part of him, which was a realistic concern because Rupert was looking at Elephant like a gambler coming off a marathon poker game in Las Vegas looks at the all-you-can-eat breakfast buffet, like he has something to settle with a tall stack of pancakes, and he's all business and all fork.

Rabbit didn't even notice. "Are you sure it isn't lipstick?"

"Does lipstick drip?"

"Good point."

"You owe me for the Twig. How about you give me that…that...steak…," – he was eyeing the grey matter cowering behind Rabbit – "and we'll call it even." The drool at the corners of Panther's mouth was a nice touch.

Nope. Start again.

After they were back on shore, they began lugging their way back to the their home. That's a terrible sentence; it's prolix: they had to be back on shore if they were lugging their way back to their home. Also, repeating the word back is not good. Sometimes repetition is good for rhetorical effect, but in this case, there is nothing good resulting from it.

And behold! Oh, crap, nothing.

When suddenly, from the sky, completely out of the blue, came a shield, a magnificent shield of bronze and gold, etched and embossed and emblazoned, and so huge it could be used as almost anything by a rabbit if he could have moved it from where it landed. It shone like the sun without the need of any light for it to reflect; it was its own source of light. If it were just a bit bigger, it could have been Achilles' back-up shield.

The other reason Rabbit couldn't move it was that it was wedged into planet Earth. That's just how it happened to land. If you want to read into this, here is how: this shield was never meant to lie flat on the ground, prostrate and prone, in the position of defeat or submission. It would always stand upright. It's like that rule about Buddha statues: you should never have them on the floor; they deserve a platform, otherwise you have disrespected them. Focus.

How could they not be awed? They never saw anything so grand and beautiful and the images engraved on it clearly meant something, clearly told a story. Unlike the repetition of "back", above, the repetition of "clearly" works here; it's called anaphora.

But guess who could pick up the shield? So he did and, the two resumed their hike until they both stopped because they had a feeling that the sudden appearance of the shield was not the result of some epic spring cleaning. Someone was going to retrieve it. The simultaneous about-face was worthy of a dress parade. They marched to the landing site and carefully placed it into the huge dent in the ground.

"Should we go?" asked Elephant.

"I'd kind of like to see the owner come and get it."

"Okay."

They moved away and sat down.

They didn't have to wait long, for suddenly everything shook, Earth, sky and their respective contents and before them stood what can only be described as the worthy owner of the shield. He whispered, "Thank you," but it still knocked down thirty trees, four bears, eleven stags, and seventy-four birds. He had seen what they did and found it refreshing; others would have tried to hide it away. He added, "This belt buckle was given to me by my father. It is dear to me."

Rabbit said, “Any time,” and there were smiles all around.

Later, Elephant said, “What a nice guy. And imagine! A whole world out there and we just saw this tiny, tiny bit of it. But just from that, we know it’s out there. That’s good luck.”

Rabbit was so busy trying to wrap his brain around the whole belt buckle thing that he didn’t realize he was home until Elephant pointed to his burrow, which he hadn’t even recognized.

Elephant and Rabbit

First follow Nature, and your judgment frame
By her just standard, which still the same:
Unerring Nature, still divinely bright,
One clear, unchang'd, and universal light,
Life, force, and beauty, must to all impart,
At once the source, and end, and test of art.

ALEXANDER POPE, *ESSAY ON CRITICISM*

Elephant and Rabbit IV: Prelude To Apocalypse! (just kidding: The Seasons)

Our two protagonists were lounging again (or still, it's often hard to tell), with gentle breezes and noncommittal clouds and bees bouncing around flowers like clowns on trampolines. Elephant wondered about things as he often did and asked his friend, the encyclopedic Rabbit, to explain or expound on every question that came his way. Rabbit must have been a teacher or politician in a former life, because even when he had no idea what the answer really was, he was able to quickly fabricate and confidently inform his student with an answer that could pass for the answer: clouds were drifting pollen from the garden of the sky; trees are built by ants because they need something to do all the time; death is change and should never be feared; time was invented so we would have something to do with prepositions; and so on.

When Elephant saw a sere leaf resting on the ground, he looked up to examine the fresh, green kind; then he looked again at the dry leaf, and up again. Under any other circumstances this would have had all the makings of a moisturizer commercial, but here it was the catalyst for Elephant's next question: "How does that happen?"

Rabbit sighed. He thought: Yes, how would Elephant know about such things, little cherub that he is? And Yes, growing old in the magical forest is not the phenomenon it is in other parts of the universe mainly because Time just ain't the same here. So many creatures don't get old; second, half of the creatures grow younger; and third, Nature had to sign some kind of contract with the forest, an agreement that it can coexist with the magical stuff, but –

unless providing just cause – could not trump the magical stuff. This can be a fine line, but luckily there was rarely a need for fullblown litigation. This is entirely attributable to the fact that, in the magical forest, lawyers are used primarily as condiments in the dragon community, including Tiers I and II, but excluding Tier III because of their dietary restrictions. And we're not saying this simply to make the magic forest more appealing; there are also no realtors in the magic forest: they're used as dental floss.

After considering this, he further considered: Elephant isn't from around these parts; he may have some inkling about – how do we put this gently? – Time's indelicate treatment of all things mortal. But why should he – Rabbit – be responsible for illuminating this dark topic? Rather, thought he, let's vague it up and present it not as life versus death, but as spring versus winter, the mere change of seasons, flowers and leaves coming and going and returning. That's the spirit!

"Elephant," said he, "you take that leaf there. That leaf as you know was once soft and green. Then that leaf was told it was time to pack it up, pack it in. So let me begin like this: Do you know what the seasons are?"

"You mean like turmeric and oregano and tarragon and saffron?"

"I literally have no idea what you just said. I mean like summer and fall and winter and spring."

"No."

"Okay. So what happens is, there are these seasons. Four of them. Very competitive. But they take turns with the weather. Summer is hot; winter, cold; spring, warmish; fall, coldish."

"Why?"

"Why what?"

"Why are there four of them and not two or six? Why not just one? Why must the weather change at all? Does it change everywhere? The same way? Is summer always hot? Or can it change its mind? How do they know when to switch? How…"

"Hold on! Every one of those questions is dumb. Dumb, dumb, dumb. The answer is: there are rules. They follow the rules. That's it. Even here, which is not known for its rules, they follow them. But if you want, I can introduce you to one or two of them. What do you think?"

"Yes."

"Good. Okay. So." Rabbit thought a bit. "We'll visit winter first, since he's close by."

"He's the cold one."

"Right."

And off they went.

Winter was tuning his banjo. Though he had a couple of chairs, one of them a dark and cracked leather, he sat on a wooden crate. On a small dark wood table were a deck of cards, a harmonica, and a cup and saucer. There was a cherry cough drop just under the leather chair, and stuffed into that chair, a book the title of which could not be identified. Another crate appeared to be used as a footstool.

He was – as one would expect – a grizzled grey fellow, old, yellowed teeth, loose and sallow skin full of sores and patches of eczema on his elbows and forearms that obscured his tattoos. His nails were the color and hardness of acorns. His eyes, though bloodshot, were black and deep. And just between us, if you put a chunk of granite in his hand, he could crush it into powder with a serene squeeze.

"Mr. Winter?"

He did not look up from the banjo, but asked, "Rabbit?"

"Yes, sir." Rabbit was being appropriately respectful. He continued: "Sir, I've brought a friend of mine to meet you. I thought you could tell him how your season deal works."

"Bring him in."

"Uh, not happening." Winter looked up and saw the trunk of the dilemma.

"Ah, I see." Winter stood and walked to the door. Soon the three were sitting on the ground outside of their host's little home. Winter spoke:

"I have no argument with Summer; she's an imbecile. Wilting. Desiccating. She requires so much effort and accoutrements to be tolerated. Fall, on the other hand, is a delight. Brethren. The Season of Reason, merging art and logic, soul and sense and sentiment and....I could go on. Fall allows you to breathe and think, oppressed by nothing, stimulated by everything. But Spring..." He grew darker. Literally, visibly. He paused.

"Every year we go at it. True to herself, she never grows up. Silly, rude, Yes, she's young, always young...." (Was that a hint of bitterness in his voice?) "And pushy. She always gets her way, which means getting me out of her way. I hold on as best I can. I know the inevitable. No fool. No fool." (He looked down at his banjo on his lap, strummed a chord.) "It's good for me, this contest. Keeps me strong. Not young, but strong. You know the rest: summer, fall – thank goodness for fall! – then my time again. We all get our turn."

Elephant found Winter very likable, which is strange because pachyderms and snow don't mix, unlike pachyderms and rabbits, who go together like Laurel and Hardy. Maybe it was the old man's skin, which looked remarkably like Elephant's. Or maybe the banjo, which he had never heard before. Or his resilience. The real reason was a bit more subtle: something about the old man reminded Elephant of the time he jumped into the river. I don't know. As they walked home, Rabbit asked Elephant what he thought. Elephant didn't answer right away; he was too lost in thought to say what he thought. He finally said, "I think I'm happy."

Rabbit wasn't expecting this, so now he was silent. Ever get struck with a sudden burst of happiness? It can be pretty disorienting, but as far as little epiphanies go, tolerable. So despite the pensive looks on their respective mugs, on the inside they were smiling. Not a bad place to leave them.

"Family!"

— Gustav Rrrk
(at the Rrrk family barbecue,
6 million b.c.e.)

Elephant and Rabbit V: Family!

Some stories don't begin in the magical forest. I know, I know. Don't say a word. Let me explain.

The very river that carried Elephant clear out of our first story, brought him right back whence he had come. Call it home. As soon as he set foot on terra firma, his mother, who was called Mother Whooshponder, bellowed with delight. She did not know her son would be returning to her by river; in fact she would have laid odds against that being his passage back, but she had waited there unable to think of a better place for her to go out of her maternal mind. Sure enough - miraculum miraculorum! – here was her dear little child, like Moses from the Nile, but bigger and without the basket. Or Pharoah. It's a loose analogy, with no usefulness to this story whatsoever. But that's how we roll.

Now, as we all know, her dear little child had decided to return to his friend, Rabbit. Mother Whooshponder, again at wit's end or, to be more accurate, Whitt's Hend, the name of their little village, determined that enough was enough and took matters into her own hand, especially since she had exhausted her cliché allowance and therefore had nothing else to say.

Mother pondered (hence the name), "If the River can bring my child to me, then the River can bring me to my child. I will follow it backwards, though that is illogical, both linguistically and travelistically. But mothers do not operate on logic, so here I go."

It takes a long time for an elephant to travel tail-first along a winding river, but eventually she arrived at her destination. Her instincts, her incomparable sense of smell, and that fact that pretty much everything gets out of her way, got her to

Rabbit's abode. She had also remembered the little detail about the Mailbox of Foreboding, so she knew where to make the left.

Rabbit thought he had gotten the hang of Big when he got used to Elephant's presence, but when he met Mother he had to rejigger his brain: his definition of Big was challenged anew. Does it ever end? he asked himself, but we don't know if he was referring to brain rejiggering or the dimensions of this creature.

So, in a case of deja-vu-all-over-again, Rabbit saw what appeared to be asteroid 3855 – Pasasymphonia to her friends – lumbering towards him. It stopped – whoosh! (hence the name) – and spoke: "And you must be Rabbit."

"Well…ah …I'm not sure we should jump to any…uh…hasty conclusions."

Just then, Elephant came out from somewhere, spotted his mother, and ran towards her. Rabbit involuntarily bounced up and down. Mother and son did that trunk-embrace thing and there was great sighing and joy. Then Mother said, "Son, it's time to go home."

So much for the joy part.

Elephant looked imploringly at his mother, then at Rabbit, who glanced up at them, then wisely began to study a clump of grass by his knee.

"But I'd rather stay."

"Heavens! Why?"

"There are so many creatures to talk to. Everyone listens. Everyone speaks."

"At home, your family, your friends...."

"All Whooshponders. We only speak to each other."

"And here?" she asked.

As if on cue, Sally Bird flew overhead and shouted out, "Howdy, all." They waved up to her, even Mother Whooshponder.

Elephant said, "See? The trees, all of us speak the same language. Even the rocks..." He looked down at Phillipe Rock and said, "Hello." Nothing. Elephant repeated the hello. Nothing. Ever see a case fall apart before your eyes? Just as Mother was about to shake her head, she heard, "Sorry. I was having a bit of a row with Dominico Snail. Dear lad, how are you? And who is this delightful asteroid that has come to visit our humble habitat?"

"This is my mother."

"Dear Madam, I see where your son gets his fine looks. Lovely to meet you." Dominico was nothing if not obsidian.

How could she not find this delightful? The most important point was made last:

"And, Mother, Rabbit here is my best friend. In the world."

This caused Rabbit to examine that clump of grass with even greater scrutiny. Funny how he had grown shy all of sudden.

Mother Whooshponder knew she had to let her son go, and by go we mean stay. After more sighs and hugs, she said she would be returning home.

"Will you be traveling backwards again?" asked her son.

Rabbit looked up: "Ix-nay on the ackwards-bay."

Mother promised she would visit. Elephant swore he would bring Rabbit to visit her as well. And with nary a dry eye in the place, we all watch Mother Whooshponder disappearing into the forest and the Dominico having the last word:

"Snail, when I'm done with you, they'll be calling you escargot! Escargot! It means....Why do I bother!"

Art is another word
for shorter and punchier.

— M. Grudko, *The Editor's Mallet*

Elephant and Rabbit VI: Art

by H. R. Libdibdryerdal

Rabbit was looking through a magazine (it was the Saturday Evening Post, February 13, 1960: despite the letterboxes, mail moves slowly in the magical forest: probably the reason that The Mailbox of Foreboding isn't all that ominous to the inhabitants), catching up on the world, when he said, "Harrumph." Elephant, who was looking through the clouds, catching up on the world, knew he was supposed to ask the cause of said harrumph.

Rabbit showed him the magazine cover. "Look what this guy did. He painted a picture of himself painting a picture of himself while looking at himself in a mirror, and on his easel are sketches of himself next to the canvas on which he is painting himself."

"Where are his glasses?" asked Elephant.

"What?"

"Where are his glasses?"

"On his face."

"But he left them off the painting."

"If the glasses aren't in the painting how come I see glasses?"

"Yes, but he doesn't have them on the canvas. See?" Elephant was right.

"Good point. Good point. There must be a reason. All these things (he pointed to the helmet, and the little portraits stuck to the right corner of the canvas, the different angles of the pipe he was smoking...) they have meaning. I took a class once."

Since Elephant was now in well over his head, he nodded that head and went back to the clouds. The sagacity of that decision is so irrefutable, so incontrovertible, so inarguable, someone should have built a statue of Elephant by the bicycle path that goes around Walden Pond.

After a little hiatus, Elephant asked, "Can we ask the guy what he means by all that stuff?"

Rabbit refocused. "No, you can't. He isn't around anymore. Rockwell. So we can't."

"Can we ask someone else?"

Rabbit thought, this is where elephant memory can be a real disadvantage: there wasn't a chance that this thought was going away. I have to find someone. Luckily, he did know someone; unluckily, he was a dragon; luckily, he was a small dragon; unluckily, he had a terrible personality; luckily he didn't eat rabbits; unluckily, Rabbit didn't know where elephants fit on a dragon's list of dietary preferences; luckily, this sentence has run its course.

He was wearing a smoking jacket, but we won't dwell on that. His name was Libdibdridyral (not to be mistaken with the antianxiety drug of the same name created by Pharmferall Laboratories, Drymouth, TN). The entrance to his cave was open, and Libdibdridyral was as welcoming as ever. "Grab a seat."

Rabbit took out the magazine and gave the short version of the above. Dragon pulled out his reading glasses. "Where to begin, where to begin. Ah. Here we have a man who sees what art can do. No, that's not right. Here's a man who sees what he can do with art. What a man can do with art to himself. See?

Elephant was rapt. Rabbit was looking at all the stuff littering the floor.

Dragon pointed with his foretalon: "This helmet. I have seen many like them. In fact…" he gestured with a tilt of his head a stack of helmets somewhere behind him "…I have several just like it. It is the headpiece of a warrior. Specifically, a dragon fighter.

"Now, this eagle above the mirror. This comes from a standard that would be carried before an army. Wings outstretched means it is about to fly off after its prey. I recall troops of dragon hunters who used just such a symbol.

"These smaller images are clearly hunters whom this man admires. His inspirations. How, he wonders, to immortalize himself?"

Elephant had never seen such a demonstration of knowledge. He said, "So, this painting is about…"

"Dragons, dear fellow. Dragons."

Rabbit added, "Isn't it always." The darkness hid the eye roll, which was a very good thing for Rabbit.

Elephant was looking at the dragon; dragon noticed the scrutiny and asked him what was on his mind. Elephant said, 'It's just that dragons are supposed to be gigantic. Like…gigantic. And you're kind of, I guess, regular size."

Dragon smiled. "You're right. I am a Tier II dragon, which means I'm not the larger kind, but normally I'm the size of, say, your average planetarium. Now consider that magazine cover we just looked at. The artist makes choices. About himself! Then he recreates himself. He has to fit.

Do you see where I'm going with this?"

"No."

"That man is showing us what we all do: we redraw ourselves, we recreate ourselves, reinvent ourselves to fit into whatever world we happen to find ourselves. Do you know where we are, Elephant?"

"In a cave?"

"Nope."

"In the magical forest?"

"Not quite."

"Then where are we?"

"We are in a story. And in this story, for

whatever inscrutable reason, for whatever impossible logic, I cannot be one inch larger than you see me. For me to fit into this story, I had to draw myself smaller."

For a long time, you could hear a pin drop.

Elephant finally spoke in a quiet voice, "You know, I think that's the best story I've ever heard."

"And it's true," said Dragon. Then he reached for a pen and jotted something down. "Now if you don't mind, I have to meet a knight with an ax to grind." Rabbit said, "Don't they always."

As they walked away, Elephant asked Rabbit what he thought Dragon had written down. Rabbit knew: "It was an idea for a story."

"How do you know that?" asked Elephant.

"Because it's my story," explained Rabbit. "Weren't you paying attention?"

Thank heaven for clouds.

I must explain, lest I be suspected of symbolism or madness.

— Maxim Gorky

Elephant and Rabbit VII: A Nameless Rider Shoots Some Horse, Plays Some Horse, Vaults A Horse, Nags His Colt, Spurs His Nag, Mounts His Steed, Fillies With A Filly, Runs For Mare, And Damn I Wish Steed Could Be A Verb, And Believe Me, I Checked

by Propensity Dilatia

But this story has nothing to do with a rider or a horse. It's about Time and Space. And it's very scientific. But without all those formulas and equations and, like, numbers.

Rabbit and Elephant had finished watching Casablanca. Why some people find this unbelievable is inexplicable: it's a classic. One of the great fairy tales of our world. (See? It's like an exchange program: we share with them; they share with us.)

Casablanca: like that's a real place.

"Where did the color go?"

"There wasn't as much there as there is here. It seems to come and go."

"Like the seasons."

"Precisely, but a little less reliable."

"It's still nice, though."

"Like the seasons."

Elephant smiled, "Precisely."

Rick Blaine would have fit right in: "I heard a story once…As a matter of fact, I've heard a lot of stories in my time. They went along with the sound of a tinny piano in a parlor downstairs..."

Elephant was transfixed for two reasons: first, the movie was riveting; second, Elephant is always transfixed. He's like Rick if you bypass the cynicism and go straight to the naiveté. "Maybe not today…but someday…" Rick "sticks his neck out for nobody," until he does. Elephant would stick his trunk out for anybody. That makes two elephants in my book, which is funny because it really is. When the movie ended, Elephant asked, "Where is Casablanca?

"North Africa."

"Hmm. Never heard of it."

"You do know you're an elephant."

"I don't get it."

"Long story. Let's keep it moving for the kiddies."

"Is it around here? North Africa?"

"It depends on how you look at it: around, near, far."

"So……"

Rabbit sat up because he had some explaining to do.

"Time and Space, Elephant. Two challenging subjects. Outside of the forest, Time is a big problem: Does it exist? How much of it exists? How does it work? Can Time exist without Change? Without Matter? Here, we're not so caught up in that problem.

"The problem for us is Space. Near and Far get strange for us when we look out at the world. Are you following me?"

"Uh, no."

"Okay, so just listen. This is the important part. Where we are right now, in this forest, we are the same distance to every other place in the world. France, Africa, Switzerland, Indiana, all the same. We're near and far at the same time! You see what I'm saying?

"No."

"Okay, it doesn't matter. I'm going to talk a little Science here. You know Science?"

"No."

"You're killing me. Science is all the facts that have been made up very, very well by very, very smart people called scientists. We don't have any of them around here. Anyway, when you have two objects in the forest, you can determine if they are near to or far from each other. But if one object is in the forest and one is outside of the forest, you can't say if they're near or far, because the answer is they're both! Always! See?"

"Got it: always both." (He really didn't get it.) "So Africa. Can we go there?"

"You can, I can't. Do you want to know why?"

"Maybe tomorrow. I'm a bit full right now." Elephant got up, found a little clearing, and proceeded to chase his tail until he became dizzy, keeled over, and took a nap. Now that makes sense.

"Not so," quod I, "let baser things devise
To die in dust, but you live by fame:
My verse your virtues rare shall eternalize…"

— Edmund Spenser, *Sonnet 75*

Elephant and Rabbit VIII: The Man in the Bathrobe, Terry Cloth.

Elephant and Rabbit were playing tag, which was causing local tremors on the flora of the magical forest. These tremors may have been the cause of a small branch falling onto the home of Ed. The sound made Ed come out. He was in his bathrobe because he is always in his bathrobe, and at his feet was his black Scottish terrier, Cookie.

When Rabbit saw the man in the bathrobe, he said, "Uh oh."

Ed started to lay it right into them. "Did you do this?" He pointed vaguely to his house.

Rabbit said, "No."

"Are you going to fix this?"

Rabbit said, "I don't think there's anything to fix. A little branch…."

Ed cut him off. "So Yaw telling me…"

"Yaw?" This was a new word for Elephant.

"Yaw."

"What's 'yaw'"?

"Yaw. U ah. Wid an apostrophe. Cripes. So yaw telling ME…" (pointing to his chest) "… ME! that YOU refuse, and I mean REFUSE to pay faw the damage you caused by that branch hitting MY house? Is that what yaw telling me right now? To my face?" (He pointed with both hands to his face.) "To ME, right now, to MY face. Yaw actually saying what u ah saying…to ME?"

Ed turned to Cookie:

"Can you believe these two MOOKS? That's what I'm dealing with here. Two! Mooks! At the same time. Tell me, am I crazy?" (Cookie was smart enough to keep his opinion to himself.) "I got to tell you, I'm speechless. Speechless. I literally can find no words at this moment to tell you what I'm thinking. Not a single word. I'm standing here with no words that can come out of me."

Cookie finally spoke. "Ed, calm down. You get tense, I get all backed up. Then we get home and your head explodes when I have to go back out. It's a vicious cycle."

Ed had grown used to Cookie's ability to speak, which had happened the minute they arrived at the forest. Back in Poughkeepsie, all he could muster was a "woof," though that one syllable spoke volumes.

Ed returned to the two mannequins who used to be Elephant and Rabbit:

"Listen, I'm no shmo. I'm big. I made a lot of spondollas in the commodities pits. Gold. Orange Juice, Lumba. You name it. They all know me. Just ask.

"You got insurance around here? No, you don't. So how do we settle this? I'm thinking two thoughts at this moment. One is you just fix the giant hole you made in my house or number two, you get a guy to do it. Perish the thought anyone should have money around here. Okay, fine, so we just fix it. Am I right?"

"Hold on, Ed." This was the voice of reason; this was the branch. "Ed, you can't blame these guys. I fell. It happens. Blame gravity. Besides, there is really no damage. I'm a little branch, practically a twig, maybe even a stem. Come on,

Ed, be a mensch. Let it go."

"Oh, now it's a conspiracy! I see: everybody gangs up on the little guy. Now I get it! Well, you've knocked down the wrong house, my friends. Look at it! It's unlivable! Hey! What the…"

But he was alone now. Cookie went back inside to poop on the rug; the branch was walking into the woods to begin his new life, liberated as he was; and Rabbit and Elephant were tiptoeing to a place that was Edless.

No place is impervious. That's why tiptoeing is indispensable.

It's a poor sort of memory
that works only backwards.

— Lewis Carroll,
Through The Looking Glass

Elephant and Rabbit IX: Hannah Bat

by Snid Spinyarnner

Hannah Bat was hanging out with her earbuds in, bouncing with the beats. She was listening to "Machine Gun Funk." Biggie was tearing it up and Chief Rocka was bringing the chorus eight-x. Bats love that pounding bass. "I live for the funk": don't we all.

And speaking of pounding bass – we're talking about the piscine homograph, now – Rabbit and Elephant were sitting by the river watching Shanz The Bear playing whack-a-fish with her kids: heads dunking, paws slapping. It was fun to watch them in their gleeful exercise in futility. You see, a bear's leg can be mistaken for nothing else, so the fish knew there were paws suspended up there in the waterless world, waiting to crash down on them. You had to be one dopey fish to get waylaid by a bear, but Nature in her wisdom made sure there were exactly enough of them to keep the bears off the endangered species list. Another example of Nature being smarter than people.

A message to all of our readers who happen to be fish: Now you know that you should be studying and not reading silly stories. On the other hand, we're really handing a valuable lesson to you on a silver platter. So, forget all that silly studying and read on.

Elephant said, "I can help them. Do you think I should?"

Rabbit answered, "It depends. Whose side are you on?"

Elephant said, "There are sides?"

Rabbit didn't answer. He was using a twig to remove a piece of food that was stuck in his teeth, which required his complete attention. So nothing happened for a while.

Elephant said, "That's a lot of food." He was looking at the pile of compost Rabbit had just dislodged. At that very moment, they were joined by our very own Little Hannah Bat. You know what's great about her? She is not attractive at all; she looks like a mix of rat, a fly, and a pig, with the worst features of all of them. (No offense to Sheffield Rat, Cornelius Fly, and Amory Pig.) But she was a very cool creature.

"Little Hannah Bat! Where have you been?" Rabbit asked, happy to see his old friend.

"You know. Around." She froze, then said, "I'll be right back." She was gone in a flash and back in a flash, returning to precisely where she had stood. A tiny bug's leg was sticking out of the corner of her mouth.

Rabbit pointed to his own mouth. "You've got a little something…"

"Sorry." She slurped and the tiny spindly leg disappeared. "Where were we?"

"I was about to introduce you to my friend, Elephant…"

"Sorry, sorry, be right back." Zoom, gone. Zoom, back. Her mouth was full.

After she swallowed, she asked Rabbit, "Did you tell your friend about our adventure?"

Elephant jumped in excitedly: "Oh, yes, the

time you and Rabbit retrieved the Cape of Wonder!"

"Cap. Cap of Wonder."

"But it says Cape in the story." Elephant pointed in the direction of up.

Hannah spread her wings. "Where would I put a cape? You're thinking of a different bat. And did Rabbit tell you about the day we returned the Up? We were awesome! That's why everyone loves us! Did you know that?"

Elephant said, "Well, I had an idea…." Rabbit was loving this, but pretended to be slightly annoyed. You could smell the baloney.

"Listen. A while back, I think during the reign of Queen Wizliggar Zizzliiz III – am I right, Rabbit? (she didn't wait for an answer) – the dirty snake stole the Up."

"What was his name?"

"Dirty Snake."

"Yeah."

"Dirty Snake."

"Yes."

"What was his name?"

(Sometimes you can't be in a rush. Let's skip ahead about ten minutes…)

"As soon as Dirty Snake had the Up in his possession, we all started dropping like flies. And that's no pun. Up is what keeps us up."

"Up keeps you up?"

"What do you think? It's air that keeps us up? If it were air we'd all be floating around, you, Rabbit, everything. It ain't the air. It's Up. Anyway, everything with wings – bugs, birds, bats, angels, muses, fairies, Cupid, Victory, Iris, Thanatos, even Hermes, the clouds…It was a mess down here. Crowded. Packed with air creatures who now had to hoof it. The shoe business was through the roof. And with the clouds crawling around, it was just dark and foggy and gloomy all around. But, who comes to save the day?" Hannah nods at Rabbit. "Yep. Rabbit says to me, let's get the Up back. He grabs the Sword of Winning All Kinds of Battles, and we bee-line it to Dirty Snake's place. Ever see a Rabbit battle a Snake? It can't happen, that's all I can tell you. Unless you're this guy! They fought for hours. Rabbit knocked out one of Snake's fangs. Then he tied him in knot. Then he spun him around. Then he put his cute little furry paw right up Snake's left nostril and made him hand back the Up. Historic! Two minutes later, the sky is full of bees and eagles and sparrows and ducks and gods and angels and fairies ...all of them calling out, 'Thank you, Rabbit!' How about that?" Hannah was out of breath.

Elephant said, "Wow." He turned to Rabbit. "How come we don't have adventures like that?"

"We will. It's just a matter of time that Dirty Snake will unknot himself. Or a witch or troll will wend his way here. Then we'll have our adventure."

"I'm excited!" said Elephant. "What a team we'll be!"

"Well, the bar's been set pretty high. You know there's a monument to Little Hannah Bat?" (Now it was Hannah's turn to act shy.)

Elephant said, "Maybe the three of us… Can you imagine?"

But Hannah had her ear buds back in and was hopping off somewhere, and Rabbit had pulled a digest out of his back pocket and was settling in to do some reading, and the only action was that of the Bears trying to sweep up some dopey fish. Elephant began practicing his lunges and parries in anticipation of the big day. Then he was somehow hit in the head with a fish. A very haughty fish, we might add.

Nothing except a battle lost
can be half as melancholy
as a battle won.

— Arthur Wellesley,
The First Duke of Wellington

Elephant and Rabbit X: A Knight

by Ishmael Counterpane (As Told To Flotilla Landlorn)

The magical forest has a lot of roads running through it. They lead in and they lead out, which is an obvious thing to say about roads, yet it seems to resonate. It depends on what you call a road; some of these can be fairly rough, almost impassable. Vestiges of roads, some of them. And they have stories, too.

Elephant and Rabbit were ambulating down one of the roads that was more like a disheveled, scruffy, unkempt path that had seen better days, when they spotted a man on a horse who could have been born from that path. It was a knight.

He was an old knight for sure, and you don't see many of those. His armor from helmet to greave, but especially pauldron and vambrace, was scarred and bent. All those plates and braces could not help his posture. His long hair and beard, grey and white, fell over his shoulders, but did not hide the many scars – some deep, some shallow, some long, some round – that crisscrossed and punctuated his face and neck. His sword, dagger and halberd were equally marked. His shield, hanging from the side of the saddle, was at the same time beautiful and forlorn. His horse, the same.

When he came upon Elephant and Rabbit on the road, he smiled. And when they saw that smile they immediately felt as if they were dear old friends. The horse, who had seen everything but an Elephant, felt an immediate kinship as well. And the sun shone and all time was one time and it was good.

A short while later, the four of them were resting in the shade.

Elephant had heard about knights and had seen a few of them either at a distance or rushing by in furious, relentless, momentous pursuit of stuff. He asked the knight what it was like saving damsels, defeating evil dragons (an unfortunate stereotyping), evil giants (again), and slaying sundry monsters (and again).

"I can't recall," said the Knight. Elephant was amazed.

"When they are over, these battles, they are very much the same, won or lost. The contest is what matters. The outcome....victories..." His voice trailed off.

"But the memories!" Elephant was grasping at straws. Perhaps he felt that the Knight needed consoling.

Rabbit jumped in. (How apropos is that!) "Memories. You can't trust 'em. Except maybe for you, Elephant. But the rest of us. Unreliable stuff. And it's not even our fault."

The Knight smiled at this. "Rabbit is right. Memories."

"Then why do you do all those things?"

"You don't fight battles to win, but to fight. If you choose only battles you can win, you are not a knight. You must choose not only battles of doubtful outcomes but battles you are sure to lose. Those are the brave battles. You fight battles for justice, not for victory. Fighting the battles you are sure to lose....

those are the ones that matter. I have tasted occasional triumph; it is hollow stuff when you behold your work. I am old. I come from the world of mortality."

"Yuk," said Elephant.

"Different rules," said Rabbit. "A punishing world, Elephant. But it has its good parts.

Rabbit pointed to the Knight's shield. "It's like that. You would think all of those dents and scars and holes would make it ugly. But they actually make it better. Who wants a squeaky-clean shield? What would be the point?"

Elephant said with resignation that came very close to surrender, "You can't win."

"You need your bumps. Just what the Knight said."

The Knight would have said something about Life being a journey, but he had nodded off. His horse whispered, "That last fracas with Miggs The Troll really took it out of him." He insisted they let him sleep, so they tiptoed away to discourse about other things. Like how dragons could really benefit from a public relations firm.

A Knight

"When I was little," said the dragon,
"there were fewer stars, and the moon
was just an idea."

— B.C. Martinmas, "The Noumenon"

Elephant and Rabbit XI: Famousity

Elephant was doing his favorite thing, looking up at the sky and wondering, always wondering, when he heard the sound of wild applause from multitudes of invisible people accompanied by flashes of light and the yelling of a single name: Wonderina! She came out of the woods into the clearing where our hero sat and she rested on a tree stump beside him. She was wearing a long sequined gown with a train that dragged fifteen feet behind her. She crossed her legs in a rather unfeminine way and took off one of her sequined shoes. "Good grief. Look how these are cutting into me. Linaeas! If he wasn't positively a genius, I'd fire him."

"Who's Linaeas?" asked Elephant. Without looking up, she said, "My footwear architect. Good grief."

"Who are you?"

"You're kidding. You must be! I'm Wonderina!"

"Wonderina? What are you?"

"I'm a star."

If he had been sitting in a chair, Elephant would have fallen out of it. A star! In fact, that's just what he said; "A star! I've never seen a star up close. You're all so far away. You're lovely!"

"I know."

"I had a feeling stars would be beautiful up close."

"We are. Most of us, anyway. But especially me. I'm the most beautiful by far!"

"I believe you."

"How could you not? I've been voted Most Beautiful two weeks in a row."

"Two weeks. Is that a long time?"

"Two weeks is for-ever! No one is voted Most Beautiful two weeks in a row! It's im-possible, unless you're me. I'll be Most Beautiful for-ever and ever."

"That is a long time."

"I know! You know what?

"What?"

"Everybody loves me. Everybody."

"I know I love the stars," said Elephant.

"How could you not? And me especially. I mean, just look." Wonderina worked her shoe back on and stood up. She swayed and spun and her sequins caught light that wasn't even there. It was dizzying for someone as fixed to Earth as Elephant was. It was kind of…like opposites: the celestial and the terrestrial; the star and the big chunk of rock; the gyrating and the fixed. Yep, definitely the opposite thing.

He wished he could applaud.

"Okay, gotta get back." She limped a bit as she returned to the hidden limelight.

"Nice meeting you," he called out.

"I know. Just meeting me makes your life better. Imagine a world without me! It would be terrible."

He imagined the vault of measureless blackness that the sky would be without all those points of light. She was right.

"Do you want a lift? I'm very good at it."

She turned around. "Clever, but I know that trick. Sorry, buster, it's my show. I don't share." She soon disappeared into the woods where Elephant saw the flashes of the cameras and the hoots of the fans begin again. He wondered what she wasn't sharing, what the show was, and how much work it must be to do it forever. I mean for-ever.

My wife is such a bad cook
that if we leave dental floss in the kitchen,
the roaches hang themselves.

RODNEY DANGERFIELD

Elephant and Rabbit XII: A Bartender Walks Into a Forest Full of Anthropomorphic Characters

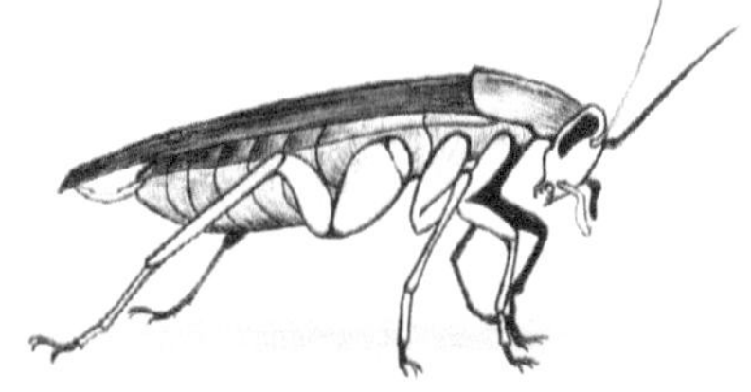

A man was running confusedly. He wasn't on any path. He was bee-lining his way towards something, but Elephant and Rabbit couldn't tell what it was. The man stopped and bent over to catch his breath, paced a bit, leaned on a tree, then started walking. Running was now out of the question.

Rabbit hopped over and kept pace with the man. "Where ya headed?"

"I'm looking for a duck."

"Well, as they say at Uncle Pete's Used Cars and Tree Bark (Ask About Our Pebbles!), 'You're in the right place.' We're loaded with ducks."

"Right. But I'm looking for a specific duck. He walked into my bar, had a couple of drinks, paid, ran out, but left his wallet. I've been chasing him for blocks, but somewhere back there, I lost 'em – the duck and the blocks and I found myself in the middle of here."

"Happens all the time. If I had a nickel for every story that began like that…Which duck are we looking for?

The Bartender opened the wallet and shuffled through the contents. "Carl The Duck. Know him?"

"Carl? Heck yes. He does wall work. Sheet rock. Drywall. Plastering. Painting."

"Great. Where is he?"

"Isn't there an address in there?"

"Lemme see. Son of a gun, here it is. 47 Quackity-Quackity-Quack-Quack-Quack-Quack-Quackity-Quackity-Quack-Quack-Quack-Quackity-Quack-Quackity-Quack-Quackity-Quack-Quack-Quackity-Quackity-Quack."

"What's the cross street? I'm kidding. Let me see. Okay, Quacka-Quacka-Quackity-Quack. I know where that is."

The two strolled along, the Bartender taking it all in. (I know what you're going to think when I tell you this: you're going to say, "That's impossible," but it's a fact that this bartender ran into a slew of familiar faces: Joey The Chicken, Michelle The Seagull, Barry The Snail, Pilaster The Mushroom, Nilla The Moth, Varella The Dragon, Mikey The Three-Legged Dog, Rippsy The Mortgage Broker, Florence The Nightingale, Richard The Lionhearted, Sasparilla The Five-Legged Bug, Scylla The Unpopular Whatever, Noodj The Parking Lot Attendant, Sal The Lighthouse Keeper, Stoots The Palindrome, Abby The Firefly, Chance The Garden Snake, Attila The Hun, Joan The Hysterical Condor, Billy The Kid, Abraham Lincoln The 16th President Of The United States, Wilson The Venn Diagram, Carmen The Box of Tissue, Herkel The Lousy Disposition, Jack The Pig, Hercule The Leprechaun, Dizzy The Lapse In Focus, Bucky The Iceberg, Learn The Guitar, Raquel The Divine, Tallulah The Unsure, Jonathan The Cynical Dean, Zazu The Traffic Light, Bernie The Crabby Monk, Nordel The Unreliable

Grasshopper, Paul Revere The Famous Guy, Jack The Button, Joachim The Parrot With The Woman Attached To His Feet, Lacey The Polar Bear, Mack The Knife, Ruben The Sneaker, Paulette The Shy Manikin, Lord Biltmore The Moth, Ed The Bound Morpheme, And The Pendulum, Maggie The Cat, Kilgore The Trout, Loopy The Noose, Bisque The Lobster, Powder Room The Euphemism, Save The Whale, Make The Light, Alex The Large, Damn The Torpedoes, Ruth The Pillar, John The Baptist, Walk The Line, Robin The Robin, Seward The Ninety-Third Element Of The Periodic Table, Shock The Monkey, Meet The Press, Mott The Hoople, Alfred The Great, Sally The Inscribed Angle, Man The Oars, Over The Rainbow, On The Waterfront, Sue The Uninsured, Kick The Van Gogh, Bump The Price, Race The Engine, Hold The Line, Pass The Ketchup, Consider The Options, Parse The Sentence.... Priests, Rabbis, Magicians, Irishmen, Frenchmen, Brits, Scots, Italians, Russians, Poles, Mormons, Vikings,

Bakers, Husbands, Wives, Old Guys, Parking Tickets. They all waved and said, "Hello!" when they saw him. They all had this connection: "An Old Guy walks into a bar." "A Parking Ticket walks into a bar." Every life should have a punch line or what's the point?)

When they arrived at Duck's house, they saw him fast asleep on a lounge chair. His feet were just touching the water in a small inflatable swimming pool. They really didn't want to wake him up. Rabbit told the Bartender to lay the wallet next to him.

"Is it safe just leaving the wallet like that?" he asked Rabbit.

"We have a saying here: Don't mess around with The Duck. He's pretty tough. Also, there isn't much crime around here. The odd Gingerbread-House scenario. The Wolf in Granny's Nightgown.

We just closed down the Straw-Into-Gold Sweatshop that Skiddly The Troll was operating."

"What's the secret?"

"Probably bribes. Skiddly has a way of…."

"I mean the secret to so little crime."

"Oh. I'm not sure. Probably all the magic around here. But it might be all the darn happiness. This place is positively dripping with happiness. Don't think that can't get on your nerves. But other than that, I'd recommend getting a place here. Mull it over. I know an agent."

"Does this place need a Bartender?"

"Even here that's a rhetorical question."

Elephant and Rabbit XIII: No

(Don't be ridiculous:
why ask for bad luck?)

One swims inside the tattered covers,
Or lurks or crawls or climbs;
One mirrors beyond,
Like a man discerning his image
on the Unbroken waters of the swelling sea.

— Hadrian Swall,
"the lowercase epic"

Elephant and Rabbit XIV: A Whale

I don't think we have to go into how a whale managed to find his way from an ocean in our world to a river in the magical forest. Talk about stating the obvious.

What's great is that this whale had been literally all over the world, the wet world, anyway, but that's substantial. He looked like he could have made the river himself through his own action as he drove inland. Interestingly, the word whale in Proto-Paleo-Indo-Meso-Montanian means (roughly) "river maker" or "channel tracker," though one singularly unromantic translator uses "water mole."

He didn't have anybody traveling inside him, but maybe we'll get lucky some other time. That would be a hoot.

Whales are the dragons of the ocean: they are so ancient and powerful that they can pass for timeless. Or maybe they are timeless, except, of course, when they intersect with humans and their harpoons; humans are the only species impervious to magic: magic requires the presence of a soul. You have to ask: who would want to kill a dragon or a whale? Even knights, who are often contracted to fight a dragon, would never do so unless a) said dragon were evil (i.e. doing bad stuff for no reason despite every effort to reason with him or her) and b) the fight were absolutely fair.

As The Whale bulldozed his way down the river, a puffin stood on his back, which is the entirety of what puffins do. In brilliant contrast to the leviathans they ride, they are hedonists: they love the wind blowing through their feathers, the spray of the waves, motions in every direction that are never antagonistic, but accommodating and mutual, never trying to usurp or vanquish, true to their singular yet conjoined destinies. The puffin embraced this thallasic symphony.

Standing on the bank of the river, Elephant and Rabbit watched the Whale and his passenger not navigate but shoulder their way toward them. Rabbit waved them down; this was a rare vision: a sea dragon. The Puffin's name was Vilchis; The Whale's name was Brindlaf, which has a kind of Nordic feel to it: makes you think of ice floes and fjords and Vikings.

Spotting Elephant, Vilchis The Puffin yelled, "Halt!" and The Whale halted. He was eye-to-eye with Elephant; each stared at the weird thing that was staring back; Rabbit in his wisdom hid behind Elephant's right hind leg: you never know with these big guys.

The Puffin flew down to the bank and studied Elephant: "Well, I have to say, you take the cake. I've been around, believe me;

I've seen squids, narwhales, sea serpents, hjaddrads, hammerheads, mermaids, jelly fish – you get the idea – but you are one strange-looking creature. And you..." (He was looking at Rabbit who had stuck his head out.) "What's your story? I've seen your type before. What are you doing back there?"

Rabbit showed himself. "That isn't the question, bird. The question is, 'What are you doing?' " which was a brilliant parry.

The Puffin said, "We're lost. Believe me, if we could turn around, we would. But this damn channel is too narrow and too shallow. Not to mention lacking in salt. And plankton. But Brindlaf here is tenacious: he'll push and plow and churn until he gets somewhere, come hell or high water, though we're clearly shooting for the latter. Any suggestions?"

Rabbit smiled. “You’ve come to the right place. Do you know where you are?”

Puffin guessed: “Brooklyn?”

“The magical forest!”

“Is that better or worse?” asked The Puffin.

“I’ve heard good arguments for both, but that’s besides the point. There are creatures here that can help you. We’ve got resources.”

“Like a crane? Because Brooklyn has cranes.”

Rabbit took a deep, calming breath. “Just Sydney, Wilco, and Cholly. Frisco is away right now. But it doesn’t matter. Wait here.”

"Like we're going someplace." The Puffin spoke to The Whale; "Hang tight, we might be getting some help."

The Whale said something in AngloSaxon; to Elephant it sounded like a cross between a lion and an angry Lexington Avenue Line Four train.

Rabbit returned with Ronsard The Pill Bug, son of Faustina The Pill Bug. The Puffin couldn't even see him, so he assumed Rabbit was alone. After that was cleared up, Vilchis spent a minute or two mocking the little guy before they got down to business.

Ronard did some silly dance and made a few hand gestures that to the uninitiated would look like those made by a driver stuck behind someone doing forty in the left lane and Vilchis and Brinlaf were one hundred miles off the coast of Greenland.

Two seconds after that – the time it took to sink in – (sink in: get it?) they were happy as all get-out, a phrase we've never understood.

No one said thank you to Ronsard, so he petulantly muttered, "You're welcome," and flew off, the classic example of that saying about small packages.

That's it.

A Giraffe walks in to a bar.
The bartender asks,
"Do you want a longneck?"
The giraffe says,
"Do I have a choice?"

Elephant and Rabbit XV: Blinky and Ned: A Parable

Blinky and Ned were a chicken and a duck, respectively, and best friends. Right from their eggs, they found that they had a lot in common, not the least of which was being hatched from eggs. They also had wings and feathers and beaks and such, and though you could hardly mistake one for the other, they felt like kin. There may be a lesson buried in there somewhere.

One difference: Blinky couldn't fly.

The advice and explanations for this was a chorus of absurdities that was in line with every other chorus of absurdities our world produces. To wit:

Robin said, "You're not focused.

Sunflower said, "The higher you go, the greater the altitude."

Tree said, "You need to drop a few pounds. Streamline!"

Mouse said, "Believe in yourself."

Possum said, "You have to study aviation. You're grounded by your ignorance."

Rickety Bridge said, "It's your approach to take-off."

Firefly said, "Use your intuition."

Witch said, "Practice. One doesn't learn to fly overnight."

Squirrel said, "You need more speed."

Cloud said, "Be the wind."

Turtle said, “Vitamins.”

Rocking Chair said, “Gravity is an excuse for the weak.”

Ivy said what Rocking Chair said: “Break the shackles of your psycho-gravitational servitude.”

Rustling Noises said, “A little Lipo, a little Botox, and you’ll be flying high.”

Elf said, “Think of all the creatures you’re disappointing.”

That he was not meant to fly was impossible, not only because he appeared to have all of the accoutrements of flying creatures, but because he had no idea what else he was suited for. He had heard barbaric stories that answered that question, each involving basting, frying and/or condiments. Of course, these stories had their origins in the unthinkable world that circumscribes the magical forest.

Was the answer to the matter of his existence nothing? And did the the nothing of his existence the matter? Was the ability to fly the solution to the matter of existence? Was Ned's existence superior to Blinky's? He wondered how his existence could be inferior to that of Kip The Stapler, whose essence was absolute and irrefutable. Kip could boast that he knew his purpose; he referred to it as his calling. His Calling.

Thank goodness for Rabbit, who took Blinky aside for a little chat. The furry guy is like a Buddha.

"I can't fly. Do you see me hopping mad about that? See what I did there? Get it? Hopping? 'Cause I'm a Rabbit. I crack me up."

"At least you can hop."

"Okay, I can hop. Who goes around saying, 'Man, I wish I could hop. That would solve all of my problems.' No one."

"Well, who wants to be a chicken?"

"Hold on, buckaroo. I thought the problem was flying. Now you're telling me it's being a chicken. Which is it?"

Blinky really had to grapple with that one. "I guess it's about being a chicken."

Rabbit smiled. "That's funny. Do you know why? Because you are a chicken. You've nailed it. No one does chicken better than you. Even Ned can't do chicken like you. And here's the kicker: no flying necessary: it's all scratching, pecking and the occasional long jump."

Blinky felt a little better, if not for the words, then for their intention.

Rabbit, seeing a glimmer of tranquility on Blinky's mug considered himself a genius: "I should have gone into sales. Talk about making a silk purse. Who the heck would want to be a chicken? I mean, a flightless bird? What's the point?"

But sometimes a rabbit's voice can carry, and sure enough Blinky heard what had been spoken *sotto voce*. "I will have you know, " asserted Blinky, "that I come from a long, storied, proud line of fowl! My great-great-great grandfather was none other than Pullum Flavorus Marinatus! His wife was the Duchess Marsalla. My great-great..."

As he squawked his lineage, Rabbit's sensitive ears literally rolled themselves into little scrolls of fur; but that's not important. What is important is that while Blinky squawked his lineage, the chicken realized how wonderful his family was; he was proud and justifiably so; and nothing could be less important than being able to fly.

Rabbit said, "Give the chicken a cigar."

"Omnia Transeunt: Gaudeamus!"

"...THE WORKS OF GIANTS CRUMBLE."
(FROM "THE RUIN" TRANS. RICHARD HAMER)

Elephant and Rabbit XVI: The Mayfly College Commencement Speech as reported by Mildew Dunfielder

(The Salutatorian – Ellie Mayfly – introduces the commencement speaker)

"Fellow Mayflies, it is an honor and a privilege to introduce to you our most esteemed – nay, revered – teacher, a Mayfly who has come to represent all that we hold sacred in our academic world, the one and only Rufus T. Mayfly! Soon, alas, he shall be adding the title emeritus to his other titles, but for now, let's give him a big, swarming Mayfly welcome…I give you Professor Rufus T. Mayfly!"

(Resounding applause. Dr. Mayfly rises to the lectern, shakes wings with Ms. Mayfly, bows, arranges himself and his notes, and look out at his audience.)

(The ovation continues)

"My goodness. My goodness. Thank you. Thank you."

(He raises and loweres his wings to quiet the crowd)

"For obvious reasons, I'll talk fast."

(Appreciative laughter)

"Dear friends. Thank you. If you will pardon the pun, time flies…"

(Laughter)

"As a dear colleague used to quip, 'Time flies like an arrow…' "

(The audience roared the responsorial: "Fruit flies like a banana!")

"Exactly. Exactly. Now I look at your faces, barely more than molted larvae when you entered college. Yet barely an hour later, you are grown up and ready to make your contribution to the perpetuation of our species."

In the audience sat Elephant and Rabbit, having been invited to attend by the parents of Fugit Mayfly, Kummwat and U. Certainly, who were (relatively) old friends.

Elephant turned to Rabbit. "One hour of school doesn't seem very long."

"They only live for a day or two, if you don't count the year they just float around like pond scum."

"So little time. What can they do with it?"

"They would ask you what you do with all the time you have."

"Gee, college really does make you smart. That's a pretty good question. How do you answer that?"

"Personally? I just change the subject. Time questions make me all itchy. How would you?"

"I don't know. I guess I should pay more attention." Professor Mayfly continued:

"My advice: As you go out into the world, enjoy it, slow down and smell the algae; follow the swarm, yes, but once in a while, buzz around on your own, see what's beyond the cloud that is us, because there is so much more. In conclusion, I end with the motto of our genus: 'Nice knowing you.'"

(Warm applause)

Elephant said, "That was good advice."

Rabbit said, "You know what? If you think about it, that's precisely what you did. You could have stayed where you were, but you decided to see the world and somehow your footsteps brought you here. I for one am grateful for that."

"Aw," said Elephant. And he gave his friend a big hug with his trunk. Sometimes a hug is better than a moral. (And there's your moral.)

Ivy comes readier without our care.

Propertius quoted in Montaigne,
"On Cannibals" (D. Frame, trans.)

Elephant and Rabbit XVII: Surly Words (As transcribed by Rent Garmin)

Shifts happen. That's what Mike the Wise Mole said. That meant that the world was going topsy-turvy until Mercury got its act together and un-retrograded itself. Big or small, everything was getting whacky, and this meant even the stuff expected to get in line, to stay in line, to make the rules, to follow the rules, to organize

structure

qualify

define

quantify

outline

present

refine

build

compound

expand

express

progress

digress

sober

straighten

fabricate scintillate

deliberate initiate

oscillate

prevaricate iterate

originate

...Yes, we're talking about those one-of-a-kind entities: W **o** rds.

No co-operation at all.

Rabbit was trying to explain something to Elephant, as always. And Elephant was listening as attentively as possible, as always, given the distractions being made by

some wanton blades of grass,

some chaotic dandelions, and

some poorly-behaved ladybugs...

Rabbit asked, "What are you thinking about?" but it came out as:

"abOUT

ThInK ? Whatwhatwhatwhat yyyyyyy

rrrrrrrrrrrrrrrrrrrr"

Elephant didn't know how to Resp... aNSWeR..... ponPLy....bbbbb
Rabbit who had a lessssssssssssssssssssssss Oh OH this is rEALLy....   " " "GET In LINeeeeeeeeeeeeeeeeeeee eeeeeeeeeeeeeeeeeeeeeee not like THat (Elephant was upsidedown now) and it was beginning to rain up.
Rab how lo it on mist

mOOn wz loffin

Sn scool d strnLY e

Then before you knew it, everything was bake to nornal.

Nature is full of genius, full of the divinity;
so that not a snowflake escapes its fashioning.

— Henry David Thoreau

The Snowflake Cameo XVIII
Supplement to E&R XVI: Mayfly College Commencement

One day Elephant and Rabbit were attempting to make a proven theorem out of Goldbach's Conjecture when out of the sky fell a solitary snowflake. In our neck of the woods – yours and mine – we have instruments that measure what we call temperature, and on the day we are speaking of, if it were taking place in our neck of the woods and we had the aforementioned instrument, said instrument would have said it was sixty-three degrees Fahrenheit. This made the appearance of a snowflake a matter worthy of Elephant's and Rabbit's attention.

Having recently attended the Mayfly College Commencement Ceremony, the theme of Time – fleeting, transitory, lingering, counted, judged and misjudged, blamed, sometimes acquitted, indifferent, cruel, kind, even beneficent, dispensable or indispensable, compared to god or gods, hated and loved, too fast, too slow, never cooperative, always antagonistic, always welcome, prayed for, never or always enough – was on the minds of Elephant and Rabbit.

They looked forward to a snowflake's take on the subject. (Yes, they knew full well that the opinion of one snowflake should not be taken as that of every snowflake, that other snowflakes may have very different opinions, that every snowflake is unique and special and so on, but a little slack, please, we don't have much time.)

The snowflake slowed her descent because she was smart. Not afraid, as you shall soon see, but smart; she liked to savor the moments.

Elephant asked her what she was doing, and if waiting for her response doesn't put you on the edge of your seat, you're standing.

"I'm living the life," she said.

"Um...."

"I began way up there, that's where a bunch of wetness did what it loves to do, which is cohere. It comes together to form a bigger manifestation of wetness. Then comes coldness and that changed me from a heavy torpedo of wetness to this little fluffy doily of wetness I am now. Soon I'll stop moving and I'll change into something that looks completely different – again! – but I'll still be some kind of wetness. Wetness is what I am; the rest, the forms and the formlessness, come and go. For now, I float."

Elephant asked, "Am I wetness?"

"I have no idea what you are, but, nothing personal, I'd rather be me."

"But you'll be gone soon."

"Gone? Never. That's not how it works."

"So you aren't afraid....of not being a snowflake anymore?"

"I know that for some creatures, shape is a big deal. I can tell you're not one of them. Good for you. And not for me, either. My only wish is that I will not forget what it's like to be a snowflake, because it's pretty cool. Pun intended. I remember being mist; I remember being rain; for me, it's the remembering that matters. You could say, remembering is where the matter is."

Elephant thought about this one second longer than Time allowed. He heard the snowflake say, "'bye" and she was gone. I know: not gone, just something else.

Maybe this is relevant, but Rabbit's ear suddenly twitched at something. "What the heck was that?" But Time had already nudged things along and the "that" was a thing of the past, which is why the snowflake made that wish.

Hwaet!

— Beowulf

Elephant and Rabbit XIX: The

by Accordia Somphalt-Likely

There are some strong characters bouncing and bounding around the magical forest, to be sure. But few are more powerful than The.

Elephant didn't believe it. "What's The's big deal?"

Rabbit explained, "He's a definite article."

Elephant responded: "Uh."

Rabbit corrected him: "No, that's the indefinite."

"Uh."

"Right. So you should talk to him, yourself."

(Enter The.)

"What?" he asked.

"Rabbit says you're a king-maker."

"Yep."

"How?"

"Look, I'm one of a kind. Essential. Indispensable. You can't get anywhere without me."

"What do you mean?"

"Okay. Like I said, say you want to get somewhere. You hear what I'm saying? You want to get somewhere. So, you get directions: 'First, you go to a road, then you make a right at a tree, then at a rock you make another right...' and so on. You know where that gets you? Lost. With me, it's a whole different thing: 'You go to the road, then you make a left at the tree...' You see the difference?"

"I do, I do."

"That's the deal. A river, a boat, a duck: useless. Would you rather be an elephant or The Elephant. Is your pal there a rabbit or The Rabbit? What does A family look like? Ask about The family and you can speak volumes. I make it real. I make the fuzzy solid, the vague concrete, anything into The thing. You will ask, 'which one?' and I will give you The Answer."

"What if there is more than one?"

"Hey, if any one will do, knock yourself out: A slice of bread. A bucket of cheese. A giant yawn. You see? And it gets worse: If today is a day, it gets lost among all those other days. But if it's The Day – and they should all be The Day, each and every one of them – then it will mean something. How much better is The Day than A day? All that sameness is bad for you."

"That's a good lesson."

"Do I have to say it?"

The

Driven by storm or soul
The wind breathes us.
Lean in, brace and bear
And push the world
Back.
Shoulder against shoulder
We laugh the good laugh.

— L. Bartlett,
"Hankerings"

Elephant and Rabbit XX: i got nothin'

Rabbit was sitting against a rock reading Tolstoy one afternoon while Elephant perused the insides of his eyelids, which is not a metaphor for sleeping.

Rabbit said, "Listen to this: 'Only much later, when they separated me from the other horses, did I begin to understand.' Ha! He ain't kidding. Am I right?"

"mmm."

"Precisely. It's like the forest and the trees. You know Butch the Tree? Over on Vassaltroch Pass?"

"mmm"

"Am I talking to myself? Butch the Tree! Vassaltroch! Anyway, he got tired of being just another tree in the forest. Just another tree! That kills me. Just another magic lantern, sure. But a tree is...what's the word I'm looking for?"

"Um...special?"

"Sure, why not? They can't all be home runs. Special. So he says he's moving out to be his own tree – which of course he already was, but there's another lesson for ya' – uproots and heads off to find some place where he can be his own tree."

"You mean he wanted to feel special? Is that what Tall-Story said?"

"Who? Tall...Tolstoy! Not Tall Story. Sometimes talking to you is like talking to an elephant. And I say this even though you're the only one I know, though I think we can assume."

"What happened to Butch?"

"Funny you should ask. Butch heads north-northwest. He finds all kinds of places where there are no trees. And you know why there are no trees? There are no trees because these places are completely inhospitable to trees! The soil is wrong, the animals are wrong, the other fauna are wrong. Is wrong? Is fauna plural? Anyway, he does not belong anywhere else. You know there are places where ants eat wood? That there is a type of air that eats wood? You know there are places that take wood and slice it up into pieces as thin as this?" Rabbit held up the book by a single page. "This is wood! Sliced up! Sometimes I get pretty angry when a character doesn't appreciate. Anyway, Butch came to his senses and came back to us. And, boy, did he appreciate things when he got back."

"Do you think that will happen to me?"

"How do you mean?"

"Well, you know I left my home and I came here. Am I supposed to go home to be with the Whooshponders?"

Rabbit was flummoxed. He had not intended to – let's face it – put his foot in his mouth, regardless of the luck that comes with it. Elephant was his best friend and up to this moment, was happy in the magic forest. He said, "No." Then he said, "No" again, because he was trying to figure out what to say after "No."

Then the obvious answer came: "Elephant, you did what Butch did. You uprooted yourself. But the difference is that you found a place that made you happy. Butch didn't. But now he is happy in the same place that you are happy. He came back; you came to. Does that make sense?"

Elephant smiled. Indeed he was happy, not at the words that Rabbit spoke, because he knew that Rabbit was clever with words, but because Rabbit had worked hard on this bit of persuasion for the best of reasons: he did not want Elephant to leave. So he just smiled.

"I assume by that grin that you're okay."

"I'm okay. You can go back to Tall Story now."

"You're not kidding, "said Rabbit philosophically, then he returned to his rock and his book. And Elephant returned to the back of his eyelids.

Water collects in the hoof prints,
Omega-shaped puddles
For a wanderer seeking alphas.

— Naomi Sweden,
"Head Lowered"

Elephant and Rabbit XXI: The Wayfarer (Really Just Some Ambulist)

Rabbit and Elephant were taking turns giving each other piggyback rides. Just kidding. But they were romping around, having a grand old time, as the sun played through the heavy foliage and glimpses of the sky yielded miraculous blues to appreciative eyes. Unappreciative eyes saw only the dreaded So What.

Those benighted eyes were mine.

So blind and dazed and dulled and impervious to miracles were these eyes that even the sight of a gamboling rabbit and elephant rendered nary a glance. This is what you call downcast, for all these eyes saw was their owner's – ha! Not owner's: leaser's, for tempus fugit pronto in the land of mortal coils – dust-covered shoes tramping greyly with the burden of overwhelming resignation down the road. These eyes could take the joy out of any picture, and they did. Some would call this overwriting; nonetheless, it was a gloomy scene, so the heavy brushstrokes may be forgivable, though they have the texture of Edvard Munchausen.

I didn't begin the journey as a vagabond. I'm not even sure what a vagabond is: is it the same as a tramp or vagrant or hobo or transient or rambler or wanderer or Hermes? We'll stick with vagabond; it sounds a shade less purgatorial, making me less of a purgatorial shade. And that cloud hanging over me: frankly, I like it. It reminds me of the pale shadow of Tantalus' tree.

They saw me first. They stopped their crazy dance or whatever it was and watched me accidentally approach them. Be assured I wasn't looking for company; they were – if you assumed there were some intentionality in my movements – in the way.

“Hello,” said Elephant cautiously. Rabbit nudged him, and I think he said something like this: “Careful with this guy. He’s got too much reality in him. He’s drenched in the stuff.” Elephant said, “Oh.” Or it might have been, “Yikes. It’s scary. Can we do anything?”

“I’m right here. I can hear pretty much everything you’re saying.”

Elephant turned a bit towards Rabbit: “I think he can hear us.”

“Established,” I said, then sat on the ground. Then stretched out on the ground. Then fell asleep. I must have been pretty tired.

When I awoke, it was dark and the two were sitting on either side of me. Elephant said, “You must have been pretty tired. Are you hungry?”

I was. They had collected for me a few apples, some grubs, a mushroom, a patch of moss, and couple of pinecones. They also had a small salver carved from hand-muddled dark chocolate that held a bouquet of Chinese pears, lychee, star fruit and an understated vanilla-infused dragon fruit; a chinois-strained mango caviar; a dappled dark chocolate ganache braided with a chartreuse-and-cream drizzle; and – as a modest flourish – gold-dusted Tonka bean truffles with a parade of strawberry gelee. And coffee.

"Better?" asked Rabbit.

"Oh, boy, " I said. "That was one heck of a pinecone."

Rabbit smiled: "Elephant has a knack for picking 'em. He has a nose for it." Rabbit thought no one got the joke, but Elephant was licking strawberry gelee from his face and I didn't think it was much of a knee-slapper.

Probably because of my mood.

Elephant realized something. “You remind me of someone. He came down the same road not many chapters ago. He was tired, too. Old and tired. A knight. But when he saw us – Rabbit and me – he smiled. Yep. He came from your world.”

Rabbit said, “He never forgets.” I said, “The world of mortality. Sure, but that’s not why I’m beat. I know that knight. Hell of a guy. Guys like him, people like that, heroes and all...noble, good, kind... Where am I going?”

“What do you mean?” asked Elephant.

“I mean, where am I going with these thoughts? Where do they get you?”

“Funny,” said Rabbit. “The knight fell asleep

practically right where you did. Must be something about this place. The shade, maybe. The trees. So maybe you're not so different: you come from the same direction, you sleep in the same place."

"You know what the difference is? The difference is, he's got things to do. He knows what he's meant to do. When you're a knight, you do what knights do. What about me?"

Elephant asked, "Well, what do vagabonds do?" This was strange because I never mentioned the word vagabond to him. Just to you when I started this off. So it was weird that he knew what I called myself to myself in the privacy of my own brain. Not that it was a bad question. In fact, it was the best question you could ask. And by you I mean I.

"I have no idea what vagabonds do, but I'm thinking nothing. I mean I think they do nothing."

Elephant smiled: “That’s what we do! We walk and talk and meet friends and strangers and we play and eat and stuff, but we’re not like badgers or birds or bees or those creatures that build stuff or collect stuff, but I think that’s okay.” He turned to Rabbit: “That’s okay, right?”

“Heck, yes, it’s okay. We do all right. We ain’t unhappy. But you. I’ve seen unhappy, but mister, you’ve nailed it. You get the trophy. You should write a book called How To Be Unhappy, written by the guy who wrote the book on being unhappy. You’d make a million. Would that make you happy?”

“I don’t know.”

“See?” said Rabbit. “See? Not even a million. No, worse: you don’t even know if it’s a million. Maybe it is. Look, this is my area of expertise.”

"What? Money? Happiness? Knowing?" I had no idea where he was going.

"Here's where I'm going," Rabbit said. Boy, this was starting to bug me.

Rabbit continued: "But it's not about where I'm going. I'm not going anywhere. I'm happy where I am. I belong here. But you...and this is my area...you need a path, a road. Not just any road, but the right one. Your path. Your road. You see where I'm going?"

"Uh, nowhere?" I was only partly being a wise-ass. Part of me was just being clever. It's a fine line.

"A joke," said Rabbit. "Good for you. So we find your path. And you don't just randomly choose one. You need to do it right. So." Rabbit reached into his pants' pocket and pulled out a tiny ball of paper, like a dried spitball. Appropriately enough, he spit on it, rolled it around between his paws, and laid it on the ground. Carefully, he untangled it, opening it up delicately and deliberately. "I haven't looked at this in a long time," Rabbit explained. He kept peeling the wad. It was a lot bigger than I thought it would be; Elephant and I had to keep stepping out of the way as the map unfolded. Magic.

When he was done, the three of us stood around it. "This is where we are," said Rabbit, pointing to a spot. "This is the road you were on. And these," he waved vaguely, "are your other roads. So." He picked up a twig to use as a pointer. Elephant and I knelt to get a close look.

"So. Here is The Road of Thought. Here, The Road to Riches. Here, The Path to Success. Here, The Road of Contentment. Notice how it parallels The Road of Discontent to a tee. Here is The Road to Glory. Here, The Path of Exile...." He showed us The Roads to Grace,

Love, Worship, Flight, Illusion, Invention, Doubt, Melancholy, Shallow Gain, Hardwon Victory, Heaven, Hell, Purgatory, Stillness, Fulfillment, Big Ideas Yielding Nothing, Small Ideas Yielding Nothing, Inertia, Chaos, Fortitude, Exaggeration, Inflamed Hearts, Sporadic Spasms In The Lower Leg Mostly Around The Calf, Spurious Arguments, Infallible Reasoning, (these two, again, perfect parallels of each other), Infatuation, Self Delusion, Epiphany (two more parallels), Fairness, Unfairness (yep), Destiny, Fate, Dead Ends, Missteps, Bent Calipers, Adrenaline, Fog, Rain, and every other type of weather that can be considered a metaphor, Curves and Drops..... Any of these working for you?"

"Uh..."

Rabbit rolled his eyes. "Great. Okay." On he went: The Roads of Belief, of Sand, of Shadows, of Ascension, of Descending, of pretty much every degree of plane on the x and y axes, of People, of

Seas, of Pearls, of Rocks, of Zucchini, of Susans, of Poets, of The Forgotten, of Forecasts, of Language, of Music, of Dance, of Trust....

Elephant was dozing. I was fading in and out. Rabbit was going on and on.

Isn't there a commercial like that?

"Is there a road of Vagabonds?" I asked. It just seemed to make sense.

"As a matter of fact," said Rabbit, "that's this one."

"Well, I guess that's my road."

"But we want to get you on another road. Isn't that the point?"

"Even you said, 'Your path, your road.' You can check. It's just a page or so back."

"No, I remember. Funny. You may be right. I don't know." He became quiet, Not a whisker moved. I asked him what he was thinking.

Rabbit admitted, "This is a tough one." That's all he had.

I stood up and stretched, tiptoed a bit to get the circulation going, to get my legs back. I said, "That's the one, I guess."

Rabbit walked me to the Road of Vagabonds. We shook hands. He offered me the map, but I declined. "I have a feeling Vagabonds are lousy when it comes to maps," I explained. He concurred, shook my hand again and then gave me a pinecone.

"One for the road," he said. I said, "You remind me of someone."

Rabbit said, "Don't give it any thought. Maybe we'll see you in these parts again."

I said, "I guess it depends on the road."

"You said a mouthful, Vagabond. Good luck."

As I moved away, I heard Rabbit call out, "What about wayfarer? Wanderer? Too much? Drifter? What about Traveler? Yeah, too general, What about...."

He was still making suggestions as the path took me down and away and around and through and falling and rising and forward and forward again.

I still didn't know if they were around or not.

— Holden Caulfield

Elephant and Rabbit XXII: Talk About Ducks

As you know, Rabbit and Elephant spend a lot of time looking up at the sky both day and night: they love all that sky stuff and it often leads to mulling. Like rivers.

"You know, Elephant, some folk think the sun is a chariot pulled by horses through the sky. Some believe it's a bird, others an eye, and still others that it's a huge ball of gas." Elephant laughed at that last idea, then asked, "What is it really?"

"Well, I'm not sure. I know it's a creature of some kind. Maybe a bird. Whatever it is, it sure isn't some mindless ball of gas. That's just ridiculous.

That's like saying a tree or a squirrel is a mindless ball of gas. Everything! Just gas! Can you imagine?" Elephant couldn't.

During the silence, a couple of ducks flew overhead. Probably Kilgore and Libby. Rabbit was reminded of a visitor from perhaps long ago.

"You meet all types in the magical forest," he mused. "Once there was this kid, sixteen or seventeen, tall, gangly with black hair except for this shock of white. It hadn't been raining, but his hair was soaking wet and the water had run down his neck. Daffy kid, a little drunk and a lot lost. He was looking for something, that's for sure. Occasionally he'd pull this odd-looking red hat out of his coat pocket, stick it on his head, then take it off and stuff it back in his pocket. There was something in his other coat pocket, though you couldn't tell what it was. It was something that mattered, though; you could tell.

"He was pale and wet, like I said, and lost, like I said, too.

"I watched him a bit, then called to him: 'Hey, kid! Hey!' It took a few tries before the kid looked my way. He didn't say anything; not anything audible. anyways, but I invited him to sit down and rest a minute. He came over and sat on the ground crosslegged, still glancing around.

" 'What are you looking for? Maybe I can help. I know this place pretty well.'

'Me, too,' the kid said. 'I used to come here all the time. I was looking for the lagoon where the ducks usually hang out, but no luck.'

'The lagoon?'

'Yeah, you know. The lake. I thought maybe

the ducks would be around, unless they flew south, you know, for the winter.'

'Why are you looking for ducks? I mean, if you want 'em, this place is crawling with 'em. But frankly they're not a big attraction. Don't get me wrong, I mean, if they're friends of yours.'

'Not friends exactly. I can't really say why I want to find them. It's just important, that's all. Funny how sometimes you just can't get your bearings even when you've been there about a million times. Maybe I'm just drunker than I thought, but I don't feel drunk.'

'You're not that drunk.'

'Say, you don't suppose the sun is going to come out anytime soon, do you? I mean, it's been a while. Boy, it's cold.'

"You know that guy that always had a cloud over his head? Joe Btfskplk? It was always raining on him, even when it was sunny everywhere else. Well, this kid was like that. He hadn't seen a ray of sunlight in years. The kid's teeth chattered from the cold, but the only cold there was, was coming from the kid. There were even bits of ice sticking to the hair on the back of his neck.

"The kid said something about the sun only coming out when it feels like it. I said, 'Actually, sometimes it's the opposite. Sometimes the sun comes out when he doesn't feel like it at all. The moon, on the other hand, does his own thing. No pressure, laid back, ya know? The sun is all business and won't give himself a break: he's always where he's supposed to be. Ever notice how when you're traveling somewhere, the moon will be in one spot, then another? Big, then small? Always bouncing around. Like a kid splashing around in puddles. The sun's like the parent, trudging through the day. They take their turns going from one end to the other, but the difference is in their attitude.'

The kid asked, 'Which one are you?'

'Good question. Tertium quid.'

'For me, I'd say I'm the moon. My parents really want me to be the sun. My dad's a lawyer.'

'My condolences. You know, you can stay here as long as you like. I can definitely find a duck for you to talk to.'

'Now that I think about it, maybe I shouldn't. It might be a letdown, if you know what I mean.'

'It would be.'

"The kid rose. 'I guess I should head back. My parents will have about six heart attacks apiece if I don't get home pretty soon.'

"He reached into his pocket, took out this big envelope and seemed surprised as hell. He slid a record from it and you could tell he was baffled. Then he looked at me. I explained: 'Ants. They get into everything around here.' I could have said genies or leprechauns or oven mitts and it wouldn't have mattered: seeing that record in one piece, he came so close to being happy...so darn close...but he just couldn't get there." Rabbit shook his head the same way had shaken it then, perhaps long ago.

Elephant flapped his ears; the thought of ants always made him do that. Some creatures seem to have been blessed to miss the point.

Art never expresses anything but itself.

Oscar Wilde, "The Decay of Lying"

Elephant and Rabbit XXIII: Lou

Lou was bigger than the big rock on which he sat; it was like a Pelion on Ossa thing. He wore an enormous Hawaiian shirt with a pack of cigarettes in the breast pocket. Rabbit sat in front of him, and Elephant lounged behind Rabbit.

Lou spoke: "So, Rabbit is it? Rabbit and...and you...Elphabit....

Rabbit: "Elephant."

Lou: "Yeah....Elephant...so I'm gonna tell you a story. A true story. All of it true. Every word. I'm not kiddin' around. (He took out a cigarette, lit it, and took a long drag.)

"So, this story I'm gonna tell you, it's true and inerestin', because it's absolutely true. Every word that I'm about to tell you is a word that actually took place.

So *because* every word actually took place, it makes it even *more* true, which from that makes it a better story than if you make up some parts. Am I right? I mean who needs a fake story? A lotta guys they'll tell you these stories and they'll make 'em up or they'll mix in a buncha lies and whatnot to spice 'em up a bit, if you know what I mean, you know, add a little somethin' to make it more inerestin' for whoever he's talkin' to, like to impress 'em. Like that."

(Another drag.)

"But this story what I'm gonna tell you, it's just the way I tell it, with no what-you-call extra added ingredients. One hundred percent true. Because I'll tell you why. Because it's so good and inerestin' all by itself, what reason would I even have to change it? It makes no sense. It's like what my lawyer calls half a david, which is lawyer talk for it's completely true or you could even go to jail for purgin' yourself if it ain't. So it's a lock. That's how true this story is. No baloney, like they used ta say back in the old days, wit' the guys from the club down on East Tenth. No baloney. Ha! Those guys!"

(Another drag.)

"So okay let's get down to business. First off, you gotta remember this story is true, so first, you gotta keep it to yourselves and not go blabbin' around that you heard this story, not even from anyone. And second, I'm gonna have the names changed so you don't know who I'm tellin' you about in case you mighta heard of these guys or maybe know 'em from somewhere, because some of them, they get around, you'd be surprised. They don't stay still in one place too long because it becomes a health-related issue, so it's best to move around a bit so you don't get lead poisoning, if you know what I'm telling you. Am I right? So you might bump into somebody and you start talking and get into some type of conversation and suddenly the guy looks up and says how'd you hear about that? And then I end up livin' in some trailer park in Pennsylvania and I'm payin' for everything in cash and my name is Bob Smith or something and I'm drivin' a Ford for cryin' out loud. A Ford car. And I'm doin' that for twenty years. No thank you.

"And right away you got yourself a problem. So say my name is Bob Smith. You got me? Do I look like a Bob Smith to you? Would you say, Hey there goes Bob Smith. I bet he drives a Ford car and sells shoes. You would think you know everything about me awready. I had this friend – we'll call him Bob Jones – know what I mean? Anyway this friend of mine says to me, Lou, I'm gonna tell you somethin': you follow your face. So I look at him like he lost his mobbles."

Rabbit asked, "Mobbles?"

Lou said, "Yeah, mobbles. You know those fancy little glass balls you flick (he flicked) and they got all different colors and like that."

Rabbit: "Oh."

Lou: "But my friend he says, Think about it: the only time you don't follow your face is when you're walking backwards. Other than that, it's face first. Which to me is not exactly news, but he goes on and says, And another thing: When you look at your face, you say a guy with this face, he oughta be a doctor or a fixer or a mechanic or a good guy or a bad guy, like that. So you follow your face that way, too. That makes sense to me because I seen this: you look at yourself and you say like what he says you say: You say, This guy I'm lookin' at, he's this kinda guy. But what my friend doesn't say is that this is a good thing or a bad thing. He only says, like a question, If you can't trust your own face, whose face can you trust?

You mean like if you can't trust even your own face? That's a toughy."

(He finished his cigarette, dropped the butt, and toed it into the ground.)

"I lost track. Where was I? Right. So now we can get down to business. Just remember what I told you and forget what I tell you. Just pretend like it never happened. This little meeting we're having right now, it ain't happening. I don't know you, you don't know me, we never even met. Who are you? You know what I mean? Because this little story has details in it that will make you think twice about everything. Everything you ever thought about even once. You'll want to think about your whole life all over again because you won't even believe it. But that's life. Better to learn from some guy's story than from some guy telling you some story who you can't even trust if he's reliable. With me at least you got yourself half a david. Ask anyone. But do not mention my name."

Not far from the big rock seven inches away, in fact – Beryl and Digger Earthworm were evacuating their home; apparently the smoke from Lou's cigarette triggered their alarm and they didn't want to take any chances.

NOTE TO THE READER:

Elephant and Rabbit XXIII

IS THE INTENDED LAST STORY.

IF YOU ENJOYED THESE STORIES,

DO ***NOT*** *READ STORY XXIV*

No, the creaking of the door
doesn't mean anything.

— T. J. Young
(When asked about the significance
of the creaking of a door
in his novel, *Escobar's Vineyard*,
at the Wisconsin Writers Symposium,
Madison, Wisconsin, 2015)

Elephant and Rabbit XXIV

Elephant's ears perked up one fine evening at the gentle sound of strumming or the sound of gentle strumming on a lyre or zither or something that is the typical accompaniment to the mellifluous voices of itinerant poets or minstrels or troubadors....look, it was some guy walking down the path with a banjo for all I know. I can't keep track of all that stuff; that path is like Interstate 77 with all the traffic going back and forth on it. Sometimes it's like a parade of characters of every ilk. Including elk. I had to say it.

Luckily, he wasn't wearing weird clothes, like with lots of colorful patches or with flowers embroidered on the sleeves or a stovetop hat or shoes that curled up at the toe. He was about as colorful as a chimney sweep. Even his ukulele was black and dull. (Yes, we're going with ukulele.) His eyes, too, were lusterless. No, wait a minute...there was some light in his eyes.

Behind him came the reason.

A little girl, a tatterdemalion, skipping and hopping, tripping and nearly falling over things that didn't exist or that you couldn't see, anyway, and not only did she not mind, those trips and near falls were part of her dance. And though she was behind him, he could see her every motion. Were she to fall half an inch farther behind than she was, he would have turned around, but she never did.

The musician stopped before Elephant and Rabbit, and when the kid saw them she came running.

Elephant broke the ice: "Hello."

The girl spoke, actually cutting off the musician, who was about to speak. "Hello. Who are you? I'm Kate. This is my paw." (Yup, she said paw.) "We're movin' on. Gittin' outta Dodge. We're on the lam. Makin' hay.,,"

Rabbit said, "There seems to be a lot of that going on lately. Coming and going and such."

"Yup," said the kid, cutting the man off again. "We're staying one step ahead of the law. They could be on our tails." She looked behind her, but the coast was clear. "This here's ma paw."

"Yes, you mentioned that," said Rabbit. He looked at the man, who said, "Howdy."

Rabbit said, "Say, why don't you set a spell," and immediately wondered where the hell that came from. Set a spell? Who says that?

"Wall, thanks," said the man. And they all set.

Elephant was pleased and baffled: nice folk, strange talk: about paws and tails they don't have, of lambs and hay, which made no sense, and the offer to "set a spell" was incomprehensible, unless you happened to be talking to a determined witch.

The musician had taken off his shoes and socks and was airing out his toes by stretching them until you could see the spaces between them. The little girl imitated it all. And of course, Elephant had to copy both of them. (And you wonder why Rabbit is constantly rolling his eyes.)

Rabbit asked how they had become fugitives from the law.

The kid said, "We rattled our cages. Ain't that right, paw?"

"Yup."

Elephant didn't know what that meant, and Rabbit suddenly had a strange feeling.

Rabbit asked, "What do you mean?"

This time the musician was up: "We all live in cages, don't we? Some of us live in nicer cages than others. So nice they don't even seem like cages at all, especially when you compare 'em to all them less-nice cages. To me, a cage is a cage is a cage and, no matter what, you're obliged once in a while to rattle them bars a bit. Make some noise, even if you might get yourself moved from one of them nicer cages to one of them not-so-nice cages. So we did."

The kid added, "Yessir, we surely did." And she did a pirouette.

Rabbit's eyes widened with a terrible realization: This is no musician! This is a philosopher!

Elephant's eyes also showed dread: "Are we in

a cage? Do we live in a cage? Is it a good cage or a bad cage? How do we get out? Do we get out? Is it better to get out? What is out? What's it like when you're out?....." He was standing now and his feet were moving as if he were walking in place.

Rabbit spoke out of the side of his mouth, "Ixnay, Ixnay. This guy's a philosopher. I'll explain later. Follow my lead." Then he said to the philosopher: "Well, ain't that somethin'! How about them apples! Good for you! Keep rattlin' them bars! hehe. We have to go now. Goodbye little girl. Goodbye." Elephant stood behind and waved goodbye to them, then they skedaddled away from the road and into the woods in the direction of Cricket's pond.

When they arrived at the edge of the water, Rabbit said, "Jump in." Elephant followed Rabbit, creating a wave that disrupted four thousand cricket-family picnics and induced pure elation in three hundred frog-family picnics. The forty-six million mosquito-family picnickers were indifferent.

As they floated, Elephant asked what they were doing, a question he never would have asked before; he would know what they were doing: they were swimming. Rabbit saw this. He explained that Philosophers are highly contagious and that Rabbit and Elephant were washing off any Philosophy that might have gotten on them. Rabbit dove under water and again Elephant followed.

When they emerged, Elephant asked, "What did he mean by cages?"

Rabbit said, "Damn," dove under water again and stayed down as long as he could. Elephant waited and asked the question again.

"Listen, that guy was confused. He didn't

mean cages, he meant....he meant..." (He searched for words that sounded like cages) ".... he meant pages."

Even in the water you could see Elephant swoon, Rabbit realized what he had just done. He grabbed his friend by the ear and dragged him to shore, furious at his own stupidity: Cages! Pages! Are they the same? Are they opposites? Then he said half aloud: "Uh oh."

Elephant asked, "What?"

No matter: an ominous sound – half outside, half inside – half rumbling, half rustling – made any conversation moot. It did not grow dark; it was more like the flipping of a light switch or the shutting of a door and it was dark.

If You Enjoyed These Stories...

What happens to Wonderland
after Alice wakes up?

— Stig Couvier

Epilogue

One second after the book closed on Elephant and Rabbit, Biff Wellington pulled into the All-In Truck Stop just off I-95 outside of Las Vegas, located exactly where Elephant and Rabbit had been floating one second earlier...if we can agree on where that one second existed, for here was the point not of intersection but of overlap of these, our two worlds. Elephant and Rabbit may be around somewhere; we only know where they were then and where they are not now. But I do know that I am sitting in a booth in the diner of the All-In Truck Stop and very soon Biff Wellington will walk in with a bundle of papers stuffed inside his jacket. He will hold the door open for a woman pulling on an uncomfortably-short skirt who is walking out with a coffee; he will take off his cap and put it back on; and for some reason he will decide to sit across from me at this booth. I can't explain any of this. I mean if you like irony, the change from pond to desert in the blink of an eye could be one. Or that Rabbit, who by any measure was an amazing Rabbit, was the one who inadvertently closed the book on the magical forest could certainly be another. He was like the mainstay of the magical forest, if you think about it. The anchor.

I guess you never know. I mean, look at what happened with Sherlock Holmes. There's another irony for you, or at least a coincidence: The closed book, the Nevada desert, Reichenbach Falls: Empty House indeed. Well, if Holmes can do it...

— T. A. Young

Epilogue

Estragon: I can't go on like this.
Vladimir: That's what you think.

— Beckett, *Godot*

Postscript

Elephant looked up. "What's an epilogoo?"

Rabbit had to focus. "A what?"

Elephant pointed up with his trunk. "An epilogoo. An epilogoo."

"I don't know. Just keep walking. Something has to open up eventually." Under his breath Rabbit said to himself, "Pages! I could kick myself. Wait until I catch up with Wellington. Where's that map?"

ONCE

I lost track. Where was I? Right. So now we can get down to business. Just remember what I told you and forget what I tell you. Just pretend like it never happened. This little meeting we're having right now, it ain't happening. I don't know you, you don't know me, we never even met. Who are you? You know what I mean? Because this little story has details in it that will make you think twice about everything.

Lou in *Elephant and Rabbit XXIII*

Bridge: The Analogy of The Imaginary Number

Rabbit sniffed. Cool air was coming in from the north. The leaves began to shudder in anticipation of growing sere, of being jettisoned by their respective trees, and of having to adapt to an entirely new level of existence. A new perspective: shoulder to shoulder with other leaves recently unanchored, now swept and tossed by this gust or that.

Elephant was trying to find a way to not sit on his tail.

Rabbit mumbled something and Elephant asked what he was thinking by way of a conversation starter. He tends to reach out when he's feeling lonely.

"I was thinking of that guy, Lou."

“The guy with the True Story.”

“Yes.”

“The one who said, ‘mobbles.’”

“Yes.”

“The one who said, ‘half a david.’”

“Yes, you know the guy. Anyway, I think he was onto something. Like, for example – yikes! I’m starting to talk like him! – the way he wasn’t telling his story was his story.”

“He had a story?”

“That was his story.”

“Was it good?”

"It was terrific! I loved it! Remember the part with the cigarette and Beryl and Digger? How cute was that? In movies, that's called combining loose framing with the pull-back dolly. You open up the frame, bring in something new to the picture, make it look random, but maybe it means something, so your audience has to think, 'What's the connection? It can't be random or it isn't art.' See? The story gets bigger and smaller at the same time. Get it?"

"Do you think we could make a pocket for my tail? I keep sitting on it."

"My point is, what Lou said makes sense. It's like imaginary numbers."

"I was wondering when you were going to bring that in. I saw it up there, but I was waiting." Elephant was gesturing upwards with his trunk as he said this.

"Well, here it is. What you do – what you have to do – is combine the real with the imaginary. You have to accept the imaginary on its own terms. You even give it a name, like i, for imaginary and just because you give it that little name, now it's real and you can use it all over the place. Imagine: you take what is literally impossible and you call it imaginary and then it becomes real."

Elephant took it all in (and by all we mean not a single syllable, not a scintilla, not a hint, a jot or a mote: nothing) before continuing his train of thought: "Because I could just tuck my tail right into the little pocket and then when I wanted to sit on my, uh, backside, I wouldn't have to try to swing my tail this way and that and try to time my sitting to miss my tail."

Rabbit did that thing Cilantro The Squirrel taught him: he closed his eyes, took a deep breath, then did a slow exhale. He realized that Elephant was one Zen son of a gun: he could ignore everything!

"Rabbit."

"Yes."

"Where does a tail end, anyway?"

"When it stops being a tail."

"But which way? What if you start at the far end, like the part that swings and all, and then you go to the part that's...um... connected? It just seems better ending up where there is something as opposed to ending in the middle of nothing."

"That's a good point. It sounds like something."

"Like leaves beginning to shudder in anticipation of growing sere?"

"I have no idea what that means." Rabbit looked around. "Should we get started? We have a lot to cover."

Elephant was thrilled: he loved beginnings so much more than endings.

And so they began.

A beautiful forest appears before you;
your light suffuses it, and makes it visible.
Your light is the sun and the moon
of this land, and as long as you are there,
it will be there, too.

— S. Bricluster

Also by T. A. Young

The Fairy Tale Book
of Bifford C. Wellington

"These stories. True? Not true?
Eh! Does it even matter?
Only that the matter is in the matter.
And I have no idea what I mean by that."

— Pico Kafka
(author of "The Trinity of Stooges")

Birds become trees, and trees, birds; stars and old men change positions as easily as changing seats. Welcome to T. A. Young's collection of stories in which existence is redefined, and contradictions are the theme. The usual hierarchy of fairy tale characters is gone - all have their say, and we relish the words equally for their wisdom and their silliness. Lyrical and comical, The Fairy Tale Book of Bifford C. Wellington is at once hilarious and profound. Among the tales: an aardvark has an accidental encounter with a seamstress, Horace the Frog heads west to find his story, and a critical snail offends The Number Three. Brilliantly illustrated by Theodore Gallmeyer.

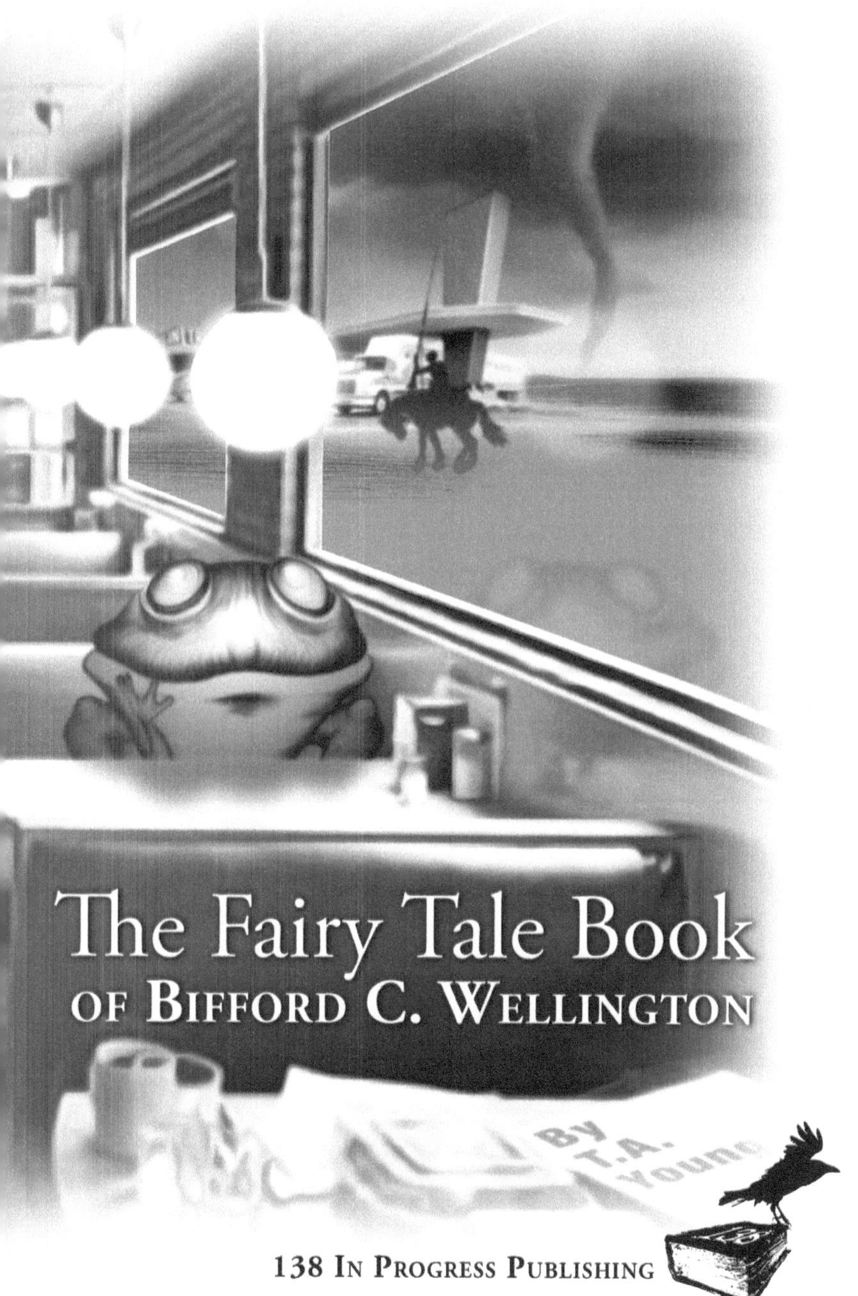

138 In Progress Publishing

www.ingramcontent.com/pod-product-compliance
Lightning Source LLC
Chambersburg PA
CBHW030530310726
48979CB00010B/1862/J

9780998276809